Look for these titles by Nikki Duncan

Now Available from Samhain Publishing:

Sensory Ops
Sounds to Die By
Scent of Persuasion

Tulle and Tulips
Tangled in Tulle

Coming Soon from Samhain Publishing:

Tulle and Tulips
Twisted in Tulips

Whispering Cove
Wicked
Burned

Her Miracle Man

Criminal Promises

Nikki Duncan

Criminal Promises
Copyright © 2012 by Nikki Duncan
Print ISBN: 978-0-9852147-1-5
Digital ISBN: 978-0-9852147-0-8

Published by Nikki Duncan
Edited by Catherine Wayne
Cover by Nikki Duncan
Cover photo by Ken Tilley of FotoImages by Ken

First publication: March 2012

Dedication

To CIS, for your constant support.

To Scott Nova, for being such an amazing cover model.

Chapter One

Bottles and diapers and…a raccoon?

"You rotten shit. Get out…" Maggie Sullivan grunted as she swung the broom, chasing an irritated raccoon through the kitchen.

Not that she expected it to listen, but the destruction the overgrown rodent or mammal or whatever it was had caused in the few hours she'd been gone had her cringing. She would get her sister back for taking the kids and leaving. Even if Grace hadn't know about the hidden cretin.

The raccoon jumped on the couch and scattered cushions before jumping to the coffee table and back to the floor in a flurry of magazines. "Arrrggh."

Maggie thought of herself as a calm woman, but she teetered on violence. She'd spent the morning in her office—was nowhere near finished with the website she'd been contracted for—and had several more hours of work still to do. Now was not the time for Jared to resume his childish pranks.

She closed in on the raccoon and lifted the broom to swat at it. *I feel like a rodeo clown chasing a bull out of the arena. At least they don't have to clean a mess afterward.*

The raccoon spun around and ran under a corner table, knocking her favorite decorative bowl to the carpeted floor with a muffled thud and headed to the bedrooms. At least the bedroom and office doors were closed. If Jared thought a raccoon made a good pet… He had another think coming.

Maggie hustled down the hall, shooing her furry nemesis. She just had to herd it to the door where hopefully its survival instinct would have it running outside. Then she would worry about setting things back in order.

Had she honestly been thinking she missed Jared's stunts? The kid watched too many *Crocodile Hunter* reruns.

Head down, Maggie followed the beast around the corner into the entryway. "About time you get there."

"It's a nice neighborhood," a deep-timbered masculine voice said from the doorway. "But leaving your door open isn't smart."

Maggie screamed. Her heart slammed into her ribs. She swung the broom up like a golf club to fend off the intruder, smacked the raccoon in the rear. It squealed and slammed into denim-clad legs.

A giant man crashed to the porch. The raccoon skittered across the man and scurried to freedom. Maggie barely managed to stop herself from spinning in a circle as her makeshift weapon flew through the air, missing her target.

With the man already down, she raised the broom again, ready to pop him. She'd slam the door and lock it, but his tree-trunk legs lay across the threshold. Still, if he made a wrong move...

She wouldn't miss again. No one would threaten her or her kids. Not if he wanted to keep walking.

"What is wrong with you?" The man demanded with a slight rasp.

She didn't bother answering as she braced herself with a stronger stance and committed his appearance to memory. Her gaze slid past his legs and over a strong, broad torso. His wide, square jaw suited his broad mouth and full lips, which sat in a harsh scowl. A bump hinting at a bad boy side marred his strong nose. Close-set, cobalt eyes glared up from his prone position. Light brown, wavy hair, still just a little too long, brushed his collar.

Crap. Chills of dread slithered along her spine. Those eyes—and the rest of his oddly intriguing face—had haunted her dreams for nearly a year.

Detective BD Harte.

His spicy scent reminded her of the cloves she sometimes

cooked with and fully clothed he put half-naked romance cover models to shame. That hard body would be a masterpiece uncovered. *Whoa! So not the time for fantasies.*

"I realize we didn't meet on good terms before, but I didn't expect to be attacked," he said as he pushed himself to his elbows.

Her pounding heart plummeted. She stumbled back, vividly recalling the other times she'd seen the man currently sprawled at her feet. In dreams, he'd sprawled naked on her bed. In person, he avoided her. Or he had at the courthouse when she'd attended the closing day of trial and tried to thank him for helping her, to thank him for ensuring her husband's killer went to prison.

Her stomach dropped like a lead balloon. The broom slipped from her grip, landing on his chest and making him flinch. "Who's dead?"

"Sorry?" Harte's brows pleated as he flicked her makeshift weapon aside.

Sorry. Maggie's shaking hand covered her mouth. He'd said that just before shattering her world. *Sorry, Mrs. Sullivan. There's been an accident. Your husband, Mike, didn't make it.*

"Why are you here? Who have I lost now?" She released a shaky breath. The kids were at the water park with Grace. Safe. She couldn't lose them.

"No one I'm aware of." Detective Harte jumped to his feet in a lithe move.

"Then why are you here?" Relief wiggled her knees and threatened to take her to the ground beside him. She contracted her muscles refusing to be weak. She *would* control herself this time.

"We need to talk." His hard, unreadable eyes regarded her as he pointed behind him. "What the hell was that?"

Startled, either by his move or the shivers his voice sent down her spine, she raised her gaze. He towered over her by at least six inches. Lean and ropey, he was harnessed power.

She bit her bottom lip to suppress a nervous giggle. How

crazy was it to find his irritation sexy? Or to have her mind jump to the sexy image of him in a prone position naked in her bed? "My son Jared's latest attempt at a pet. Is my family safe?"

"As far as I know, yes. Why don't you get the kid a fish?"

"They keep dying." His presence scared her, but she remembered tenderness. The way he'd held her. And he'd gotten right to the point of delivering the bad news. He was alert and edgy, but not as foreboding as last time. He wouldn't be talking about fish if something had happened to her family. She sagged against the wall as her mind settled.

"Suicide," Harte muttered. "Smart fish."

"What are you doing here, Detective Harte?" As soon as the words left her mouth, his slightly cynical smirk slid away to a flat, blank look. Her throat tightened, her stomach jittered, her heart hammered.

"I need to ask you some questions, Mrs. Sullivan."

"About...?" *Something that's going to screw up my life again.*

Harte stood on the threshold and looked over her shoulder into the living room, clicking his tongue. "Raccoon do all that?"

"Yes." Maggie looked over her shoulder at the havoc. She twitched and turned away. The image wouldn't budge from her mind. "What questions?"

Harte leaned back and looked briefly down the street, clearly wanting to be somewhere, anywhere else. "Can I come in?"

Get to the point already! "Sure." She led the way into the living room, which resembled a hurricane's path, and motioned him toward a chair. She straightened the scattered pillows on the sofa and sat. Five minutes. He could have five minutes before the mess made her skin itch with the need to clean it.

"There's been a death in the park down the street. Would you mind looking at a photo for me?"

Murder. Homicide detectives didn't go door to door for a

natural death or an accident. She braced herself for the possibility of seeing someone she knew, cared for. She already knew the feeling of tragedy. While hoping she wouldn't know the victim, she felt horrible for anyone who did. "Okay."

He reached into his jacket and pulled out a photo. "Do you know this woman?"

It was a headshot. Closed eyes. Colorless skin.

"No. She looks like me." Her skin crawled. Hadn't she dealt with enough death? And this had been close. Too close.

"Not really." He cleared his throat.

The once beautiful woman was lifeless. Her pain and horror-filled eyes stared straight at the camera. A purplish discoloration marred her left cheek. "Who is she?"

"We believe her last name is Dane. We're hoping someone in the area might know more."

"Sorry. I don't know her." Maggie's throat ached with sadness and remembered grief. The woman's family would soon face the helplessness and devastation of loss. The unanswerable question *why* would taunt them.

Time dulled the gripping pain, but it never seemed to go away. Even the shared grief and support of her own family hadn't eased Maggie's agony. Her relief had come when Detective Harte had held her and offered condolences. His words had been the same he likely offered to anyone else, and though he'd seemed to intimately understand what she'd face, as if he'd faced similar loss, she'd gotten the impression he didn't make a habit of comforting family members left behind.

"What happened to her?"

"We're not releasing details at this time."

"Right." She was sorry. Sorry he'd brought death to her door again. Sorry a woman had suffered a blatantly agonizing end. Sorry she couldn't identify the woman who deserved to have her full name in death.

Maggie shook her head and handed him the photo. "I've never seen her."

"Have you noticed anything, anyone, unusual around the

neighborhood lately?"

"Aside from a black car with dark tinted windows that occasionally drives by?" She leaned forward and straightened the magazines still on the table. Time was running out on the minutes. "No."

An odd look crossed Harte's face as he tucked the picture in his pocket and pulled out his notepad. "Can you be more specific about the car?"

"A new Audi. Four door. Black. Expensive looking black rims."

His pupils flared briefly before he looked down at the notebook. "That's pretty specific."

"Jason Statham drove the same thing in the second *Transporter*."

He nodded slowly in apparent appreciation, either because she knew her cars or watched action flicks. "So it isn't a neighbor's? Maybe someone's company?"

"Not unless a visitor rolls past my house at idling speed without slowing at anyone else's home."

"How often does this happen?"

"Once a week at least. For the last several months." At least that's when she'd noticed it thanks to new sleeping habits.

"You notice quite a bit." Harte jotted notes without looking up. "Did you catch the plate number?"

"I don't sleep much. And no." The base of her spine itched with awareness of him as a man, but also with knowledge he was holding something back. What? Why?

"Thank you for your time." He stood to leave, pulled a card from his pocket and offered it to her. "Please, let me know if you think of anything more."

She glanced at the card before meeting his gaze. "I have your numbers."

Call if you need anything, he'd said a year earlier as he placed his card on the console table. She'd thought of reaching out a time or two, but doubted he'd really intended to make the offer. Still, his card was tucked into her personal phone book by the phone.

"Right." He cleared his throat and slid the card back into his pocket. "Well, let me know if you see anything. I'll see myself out."

"Sure thing." She nudged a few magazines aside with her foot and followed him.

"Hey." He turned with his hand on the knob. "Wasn't your husband a professor?"

"He was a linguist. He taught at University of Texas at Dallas." Why would he ask that? Was there a connection?

Harte nodded as he pulled open the door. "Thanks again for your time, Mrs. Sullivan."

"I wish I'd been more help." She followed him onto the porch and fought against the images of her breaking under the weight of searing agony. The grief and pain she'd thought had eased flooded back tightening her chest and throat in sympathy for an unknown family. She couldn't shake the thought something big was about to disrupt her world.

"I hope you find your answers."

Maggie watched Harte's arresting and confident stride as he crossed the lawn toward a black Audi. He was halfway to his car when she called out to him. "Detective! About the car I mentioned."

He stumbled as if the ground had jumped under his feet. "Yeah?"

"It's remarkably similar to yours." She tilted her head and looked past him. "Right down to those rims that perfectly match the paint job. They're more subtle than traditional ones, which is what makes them noticeable."

"Interesting." He nodded and continued toward his car without looking back.

Yeah. Interesting. Why had Detective Harte been checking up on her?

On the other side of the parking lot of the vacant

warehouse, a man sat in his late model Monte Carlo with the engine idling. Adalia pulled in and stopped her van several car lengths away.

Anticipation of finally stopping the bitch surged even as BD instinctively worked to keep his breathing level. Before he could react or move in, Adalia shifted her hands on the wheel and then gunned the gas.

Faster than her van closed the distance to the waiting man realization struck. Someone wouldn't be going home.

Without remembering the details of his actions, BD raced to Mike Sullivan's car. He sat with the man struggled to breathe with a shard of windowpane protruding lethally from the side of his neck. The man's every labored breath pumped another spurt of blood onto his pristine shirt.

"Take care of Maggie. Promise."

BD jerked himself out of the quicksand memory before it sucked him into a darker void. It was hard enough fighting free of the nightmare each morning. He didn't need it during the day.

"This goes back to however she was involved with the husband." He pulled on a pair of boxing gloves and headed for the punching bag. "Any word on when and how Adalia escaped?"

Craig Harrison, his partner and best friend since childhood, took his position on the other side of the bag to hold it still.

A year earlier they'd arrested Adalia Wood after she'd driven into his car to make sure he didn't talk about whatever he had been meeting her for. She'd brutally killed several people and left taunting notes at each scene. Her methods of torture and murder were so varied they'd only connected them by her constant use of an ivory stationary with a Gryphon watermark.

"Middle of the night," Craig said. "There are gaps in the intel, but she had to have help."

"Son of a…" *Punch.*

"Say it. You won't offend my virginal ears."

He glared at Craig. "Help like before?"

They'd suspected she had an accomplice, but had been unable to find anyone connected to her. She was smart, incapable of showing genuine sympathy to another person, and completely isolated in her world. Male victims saw her as a beautiful woman in need of saving. Female victims regarded her as a friendly acquaintance. No one they had interviewed had been able to do more than describe her appearance. She was most dangerous because of her ability to blend in.

"Not sure." Craig planted his feet more firmly. "Wood's cell mate confirms that she's targeted Sullivan's widow, but doesn't know why.

"A fight broke out sending several inmates to the infirmary. She was stabbed and disappeared when the responding ambulance took her to a hospital for surgery. The warden is emailing a scan of Wood's file and visitor logs."

BD grunted as he landed another punch. He'd suspected Maggie was going to be involved when he saw the body in the park. He'd known it when she confirmed her husband had been a professor. What he couldn't figure now any more than he could then was the connection between Mike Sullivan and Adalia.

Maybe an affair, but somehow that didn't sit right in BD's gut. It wasn't a strong enough reason for a woman like Adalia to kill a man or go after his wife a year later.

Regardless, death was back at Maggie's door and he had a promise to keep. The potential ramifications of spending time around her had pressure building at his temples. She'd pulled at him, sexually and emotionally, when he'd shattered her world. Her allure had grown with time, judging by his earlier reaction.

"What good does it do to put murderers behind bars if morons let them go?" BD ground his teeth. They had to redo a job they'd already done because of incompetents.

Punch. He'd prefer himself or Craig being the targets. They were trained.

A target on Maggie... He may as well have been gut punched by a three-hundred-pound thug on a high. He didn't stand a chance of blocking the force of such a hit any more than he could remain unaffected by the exotic looking widow with her dark hair and compelling gaze.

Adalia was crafty and planned everything ten moves in advance, which meant BD was going to have to get close to Maggie. She needed protection and sitting in his car each night wouldn't be effective.

"Adalia mentioned a professor in the note on Michelle Dane." Thankfully they'd identified the woman in the park. "Maggie's husband was a professor, but what's the logic behind targeting her?"

"Vindication?" Craig ventured. "Maggie was at the trial for most of the closing statements. Women can latch on and turn small grudges into vengeful ones."

"No." BD slammed his fist into the polycanvas bag. "Family members of her other victims were there too. They haven't been identified as targets."

What did Mike Sullivan have to do with Adalia? What hat she wanted to keep him from talking about? She wasn't crazy. She had reasons for every action—even if BD couldn't pinpoint them.

Craig braced the bag and studied him. "She got to you again."

"Maggie?" *Punch.* "No." *Yes.* Seeing her threw him back in time. He recalled every emotion crossing her face when he told her he was responsible for her husband's death. That had been the second time he'd failed to react fast enough. Nothing would distract him this time.

"BD—"

Punch. Ignoring the suspicion in Craig's tone, BD jerked his head. He'd have to put more into his punches if he wanted to move the bag. Moving Craig could be like moving a mountain.

"She dressed more primly today, but I still see her in

16

Pepto-Bismol pink cleaning gloves with a rip in her jeans and her chin jutted out in defiance."

Her house had been cluttered with kid stuff last time he'd been there and her hair had been in a messy ponytail. Aside from photographs in decorative frames of a relaxed Maggie and the mess from the raccoon, she now portrayed an obsessively controlled person. Nothing in her life was allowed to slip from its approved slot. She hadn't even been able to look at the magazines on the table without straightening them.

Punch. Facing her again ripped open old wounds and awakened the memory of her body pressed against his. His heart trembled with the echoing memory of her pain.

"She's a job." *PUNCH.*

Craig grunted and stepped back with his right foot.

Punch. Punch.

"Right." A job and nothing more. So why had he avoided women since meeting her?

Yeah, his thoughts about the widow were inappropriate. The temporary—and intense—attraction he'd felt while offering comfort to a grieving woman made him the lowest kind of sleaze. Damn if he hadn't felt a stronger attraction today.

Her pleated slacks and silk tank top accentuated her curves. Elegance radiated from her even as she chased a raccoon with a broom, and the instinctive attempt to take him down when he'd startled her… Her spirit was arousing.

"That case was tough for you."

BD pictured Adalia's face and put the full weight of his body into the next swing. *Punch. Punch.*

He knocked Craig back two steps. Bouncing on his feet, BD rolled his shoulders. That felt good.

"I did what I needed to do to stop a murderer." *And a man lost his life, a kid his dad.*

Craig stepped over to the open mat in the middle of the floor and held his hands out to his side in invitation. BD pulled the Velcro on his gloves with his teeth. Maybe hand-to-hand against Craig would release the need to throttle someone. He couldn't ask for a tougher opponent.

Shaking his arms, then legs, loosening his muscles, BD stepped in front of Craig and assumed a defensive stance. He'd gotten good at defenses. Even if he didn't clear his mind, he might sweat out some aggravation.

Craig swung a test punch at his face. "And then you took it further."

BD swooped in. He landed a right jab to Craig's chest sending him back a step. He had twenty pounds on Craig and should be able to knock him flat on his see-all-hear-all ass.

"I promised her husband I'd tell her he loved her." *Promised to protect her without knowing what or who from.*

"You didn't promise to comfort her."

Anger ran off him with the sweat, but nothing washed it away. Craig had no right to question his actions, even if he was the closest thing to a brother BD had.

"What's that supposed to mean?" He spun and aimed a kick at Craig's head.

Craig raised his arm and blocked the blow with little effort. "It means you went above and beyond. *Way* beyond."

"I did what I had to." *Liar.* He had wanted to turn away from her, but guilt had sent him to her side. The desire to hold her while she grieved had made him stay. Nothing could have erased her pain, but maybe he'd helped a little.

He circled Craig, looking for a chink in his guard. Unpredictability and the challenge of finding a defense flaw, of out-thinking a worthy opponent, made the sparring effective.

"Holding the widow while she cried after emptying her stomach?" Craig cleared his throat in an unspoken I'm-not-buying-your-story way. "Was that what you had to do, or did it just make you feel more like a hero?"

He found his opening. BD dropped to the ground, swept Craig's legs out from under him. He flipped up and out of reach before Craig's back smacked the mat. Dancing from foot to foot, he waited for Craig to get back up. "What else was I supposed to do? Leave her? Walk away? Ignore that she hurt? That I'd just destroyed her life?"

"Most would." Craig jumped to his feet. "And you didn't destroy her life."

Walking away would have been normal. No one would have thought less of him, but thinking of Maggie grieving on her own... One look at the naked grief in her eyes and the option of walking vanished.

"Bull." BD ignored the sweat dripping into his eyes, switched his lead foot and swung some slow punches in the air. Craig's badgering actually had some of his anger draining away. "Sullivan wasn't a criminal. If I'd gotten to Adalia faster, he wouldn't have died."

"You seemed awfully protective of someone who was just a victim's wife." Craig raised a brow, practically daring BD to try another move. He'd assumed his role as pseudo-therapist, encouraging BD to talk about his feelings. "She reminded me of Sam."

"No way." BD envisioned Maggie as she'd been in the courtroom. Dressed in a somber gray suit, sitting statue stiff with a blank stare, she hadn't shown a hint of nerves or emotion.

Samantha had always been unable to sit still for two minutes. She had been outrageously and overtly sexy. Her bravery ended at trying a new shade of nail polish. Maggie Sullivan was quietly sensual and aside from soft clothes didn't seem the least bit fragile. Especially with a broom in her hand.

BD swung at Craig again, but was easily blocked. "We may be men, but you can still talk about your feelings."

"No."

"You keep this close-minded caveman act up and Cap will assign someone else to the case, though maybe that's for the best."

Chest heaving, teeth grinding, a fire-burst of temper propelled BD into Craig. Grabbing his best friend by the shirt, BD slammed him into the wall and got in his face.

"Adalia Wood is ours. Mine. If Maggie needs protection *I* will see to it." He pressed Craig harder against the wall. "You open your meddling mouth to Winchester and I'll personally pull your balls out your throat. Then we'll talk about *your* feelings."

"You can try." A cocky grin spread across Craig's mouth. "After you get your head straight."

An hour later, while they worked at dissecting everything in the case files from their first go-round with Adalia, BD still fumed over Craig's hard view of his actions. Again they tried to find a logical connection between her victims aside from the cryptic notes left with the bodies.

"Why was she so direct in her last note? She was more vague before." Craig twirled a pen between his fingers. "And what's she mean by 'our failure resulting in mass destruction'? How many people does she plan to kill?"

"I don't intend to find out the last answer. As for her directness, maybe she's working against a timetable. Or she's grown impatient, which will make her screw up. We just have to figure out her agenda."

Craig looked up from the paper he was reading. "We have to tell Mrs. Sullivan."

"No." BD could see it now. Him explaining to Maggie how the woman sentenced for Mike's death had escaped, killed another woman and that Maggie may be next. Of course he couldn't forget the part about her husband maybe being involved with Adalia.

"No," he said again. "It wouldn't go over well."

"She'll be safer if she knows."

"Or she'll go off half-cocked thinking she can handle the situation." BD pinched the bridge of his nose in an attempt to alleviate some of the pressure. While there was nothing fragile or timid about Maggie, she wouldn't take orders well—even for her own protection. "We need a way to stay close without her knowing what's going on."

"We've upped patrol car presence in the area."

"Which won't be enough." Wood was too clever and always a step ahead. "We'll need to take turns watching her house at night."

"Have I mentioned my hatred of stakeouts?" Craig, the mellow member of their team who dealt more easily with periods of inactivity as they related to doing paperwork hated sitting in a car for hours. Where Craig thrived on mental stimulation, BD fared better when his mind could drift from possibility to possibility.

"Loan me your car. I'll cover them." It was a better option than going home to the cheap, pre-furnished apartment he'd moved into after Samantha.

"Why do you need my car? What's wrong with yours?"

BD leaned back in the chair and rolled his neck. "Maggie identified mine from a few sweeps I've done. If I park all night she'll know something's up."

Craig's left brow popped up. The pen rolled seamlessly through his fingers like a miniature baton. "Man, where to start. How about with pointing out she's already aware something's up?"

"Been there." BD tapped his temple and ignored the sarcastic air quotes Craig framed "something's up" in.

"You take the fun out of it when you don't fight back. Well…" Craig grinned slowly, only raising one side of his mouth. "Mostly. That you've been checking up on her and keeping it secret…" The weight of what Craig didn't say sat like boulders on BD's mind. "How long's it been going on?"

"Awhile." Three more days would make a year. Not that he'd counted.

"Okay. She's observant. Probably too much so to be fooled with a different car. If anything it could scare her into calling 9-1-1."

He'd thought of that too.

"I'm open to alternatives." As long as they didn't involve being close enough to smell her sweet scent of vanilla and roses.

"You want her to be careful? Give her a reason. Her concerns will be raised and she'll stay on guard."

"A warning won't keep her safe from Adalia."

Thinking, Craig flipped the pen back and forth three times before tapping it on the desk. "You could date her. And don't think I've missed that you're ignoring my question."

Date her? Maggie was sensual and had a quick wit. As he'd been sprawled on the porch, with her standing over him, erotic images had flashed in his mind of her naked, lowering herself onto him. Of her hair falling loose from her braid in soft waves over her shoulders. Spending time with her wouldn't be a hardship.

Yes it would. "I need to be close, but dating her isn't going to work."

"Because...?"

"It takes time we don't have. And it doesn't get us close enough." Maggie and her son wouldn't be safe enough.

Craig snapped his fingers. "There's an empty house next door. Maybe we could talk the owner into letting us rent it for awhile."

"Thanks to the economy and budget constraints, Cap won't release funds." Which left BD with the options of watching her house from the car or pretend dating her. There had to be an approach less littered with buried bombs.

Chapter Two

Maggie put a finally sleeping Emma in her crib and went to check on Jared, who was sprawled on his stomach across his bed with his feet dancing in the air above him. "You're supposed to be cleaning your room, not playing DS."

"Almost done with this level."

She closed her eyes for a brief moment to hold her frustration in check. Jared's behavior would be easier to handle if he was intentionally defiant for the sake of gaining attention. Instead, he had retracted so deep into himself, stopped acting like a typical young boy, she worried he might be borderline depressed. He had fun with his friends, he'd pulled a few small pranks again, but grief over losing his father still shadowed him. And he never smiled.

"When you finish that level, get your laundry picked up and into the laundry room. Or you won't need to worry about the next level."

"Yes, ma'am."

She pulled his door closed and headed out for the mail, wondering yet again if she should still be allowing him to slide by without ever fully cleaning his room. In the grand scheme it wasn't the most important thing. He would come around eventually, unless her leniency made him too complacent.

The mess still drove her crazy, crap it made her skin itch, but Grace, a psychiatrist, insisted it was best left alone and had promised Jared's reactions were normal. Before much longer she'd have her high-spirited, laughing, prank-pulling son back in full force. The raccoon from a couple days ago hadn't gone over well, but it was a sign he was bouncing back.

If only he could dream up less destructive pranks. Shaking her head, Maggie flipped back the deadbolt and pulled open the door.

The metallic stink of blood rose. A scream surged up and

lodged in her throat. Her stomach rolled. She jerked back a step.

The raccoon she'd chased out of her home lie on the welcome mat—gutted. Violated. He'd been sliced open from the furry white star at the bottom of his chin to the base of his tail. A piece of paper protected by a plastic bag was stuck to the creature with a knife.

Curious, Maggie squatted down to grab the bag, but instead left it untouched and held her breath while looking more closely.

The paper had the University of Texas at Dallas logo. The woman from Detective Harte's picture smiled up from the page.

Michelle Dane, according to the name beneath the enlarged photo ID printed by one of Mike, had been stunning. She had been a linguistics professor who had been Mike's replacement if the dates of employment printed beneath each picture were accurate. The paper read like tombstones.

Maggie's blood chilled. The woman in the park. Detective Harte's visit and drive-bys. Now the raccoon and pictures. She was no Sherlock Holmes but one of these things shouldn't fit with the others. Yet it seemed to. She scanned the surrounding houses before stepping back and closing the door.

Striving to be calm, wishing her shaking hands would get the message, she pulled out Harte's card. She hadn't expected to see him after he'd walked away from her at the courthouse. She'd half hoped not to see him again after his latest visit. She sure hadn't expected to be dialing his number.

Massaging her flip-flopping belly, breathing slow in an attempt to calm her quivering heart, she braced herself for the shivers the deep timber of his voice caused. As if she needed more shivers. He carried himself with a confidence that promised the passion she'd always yearned for. The passion she imagined would make her feel alive.

Detective Harte was not the man to test the theory on. He was dangerous, with a deadly job. And her traitorous body heated up just thinking about him. Being in a room with him exaggerated the issue—a scary predictability.

Mike's job had been predictable and he'd still been killed. A detective was in danger daily. She couldn't live with the doubts and fears. Not that it was an issue. They weren't having a relationship. "Get a grip, Maggie."

She had her life in order. She didn't need or want a relationship. She had her hands full being mom and dad to two kids.

"Detective Harte's desk." A hard, disapproving voice pulled her from her thoughts. "Detective Pritchett speaking."

"Is Detective Harte available?"

"Well now, sugar," the detective purred. If slime-coated arrogance could be a purr. "Why would you want Harte when I can satisfy your needs?"

"Um..." Her skin twitched with instant revulsion. Never before had a voice on the phone made her feel as violated. She'd rather clean up the raccoon herself than talk to this guy. "I called for Detective Harte."

"You can't do better than me." Smarmy satisfaction slithered along his tone like a laugh. "Can't I help you, darlin'?"

Keeping her disgust disguised would be a challenge, it sat so thick on her tongue, but she tempered it. "I'll call his cell."

"You don't know the pleasure you're missing."

She hung up and stared at the silent phone in her hand for three seconds before a full body spasm shook her. "Ugh. What a sleaze."

Grateful she hadn't met the detective personally, she dialed Harte's cell. It rang once before his deep voice vibrated into her ear—effortless and arousing, a truly genuine purr that belonged on sex lines.

"Detective Harte."

At least someone knew how to answer a phone. "It's Maggie Sullivan."

"What can I do for you?"

"I received a delivery you should see."

"What?" The professional inquiry he'd led with became a terse one-word snap.

"I would prefer it if you came over." The raccoon image was planted firmly on her memory, but she'd rather not describe it. "It's on my porch."

"We'll be right there." He said something in a muffled voice, then spoke directly into the phone again. "Keep your broom in the closet." *Click.*

She held the phone away from her ear and rolled her eyes. What was it with cops? Did their mothers not teach them any manners? Or did the academy erase the training?

She checked on Jared, told him to stay in his room and listen for Emma. He nodded and kept playing his game. She headed back to the entryway to watch for Harte out the front window, but he and his partner were already on the porch.

They were dressed similarly in jeans and snug, muscle-hugging T-shirts with lightweight suit jackets likely intended to conceal their guns. Harte's partner, Craig if she remembered correctly, took pictures while Harte ordered someone on the phone to come deal with the animal. He hung up, slipped the phone into one pocket and pulled a pair of latex gloves from the other. He lifted the paper from the carcass. His body stiffened.

She wasn't sure how to define the look on his face, but violent rage was mild.

Rather than spy on them, and she had no desire to see the raccoon up close and personal again, Maggie moved into the living room, certain they would ring the bell when they were ready to talk. The flickering images of the animal, of Harte stiffening, of the dead woman's once happy face kept her alert. Incredibly alert.

She fluffed and straightened the pillows. Turned a few of the knick-knacks on the entertainment center back in order. Looked around the room for something else to do and settled on straightening the magazines before she realized she was fidgeting. She never fidgeted.

Determined to stop, she sat on the sofa and flipped through the parenting magazine still in her hand. The doorbell rang, jarred her from her skimming. BD and his partner stood on a bloodstained doorstep, free of the dead animal.

Handsome in a classic blonde, sexy-guy-next-door kind of way, Harte's partner would likely be the charmer of the duo. His flirty smile and half wave of greeting confirmed it. She'd bet he could break a woman's heart without her feeling a moment of pain.

"Mrs. Sullivan." Harte's hard gaze roamed her face. Her temperature shot up. "You may remember my partner, Craig Harrison."

"Yes. Come on in." She shook Craig's hand and was a little stunned to find herself smiling at him, considering the reason for their visit. Definitely a charmer. She nodded toward the smear of blood on the porch she'd have to clean up soon. Very soon. "Thanks for coming so quickly and taking care of that."

"Thank you for calling us." Harte held up the plastic bag with the pictures as they moved inside. "Hopefully this will lead us to answers. Miss Dane's family deserves closure."

What about mine? Why was Mike's replacement killed? "So you identified her already?" Maggie closed the door against the summer heat and humidity. When she moved up beside Harte, his eyes were riveted on the once again clean living room.

"Yes. You clean up quickly."

"Yes." She would have preferred sleep, but until four thirty a.m. the last two nights she'd alternately cleaned and checked on the kids and watched the street for Harte's car. He'd been pretty well hidden behind a neighbor's sedan, but she'd spotted his black Audi.

Each time, an edgy flurry had spread through her at the sight of his car, encouraging her to go ask why he was watching her house and how long he'd been doing it. Another part wasn't sure she wanted the answer. Especially now.

She led them into the recessed living area. "I don't know who would have left that on my porch. Neither can I help but wonder what kind of message the picture is supposed to be sending. What does this have to do with me?"

"I couldn't say." Harte's face remained void of emotion, but his tone stated the lack of answer was due more to job commitment than lack of suspicion. Craig shot a quick surprised glance at his partner, but veiled it instantly.

"Of course not," Maggie muttered.

Harte asked questions along the lines of those he'd asked Saturday. Only this time they were more focused on her and any possible enemies. As if she'd done anything as a single mom who builds websites to make enemies. When she said as much, he suggested the heat of the summer and the inactivity of school not being in session, kids got bored and pulled pranks. She knew bored-over-the-summer kid pranks. This was no prank.

They wrapped up the questions and headed toward the door. "Thanks again for calling me."

"Didn't have a reason not to. Oh…" She met Harte's gaze wanting to make sure he understood her coming point. "When you get back to the station, you might mention a thing called professionalism to Detective Pritchett. While your phone manners aren't great, his are appalling and could land him or the Dallas PD in a lawsuit."

"What did he do?" Harte's jaw hardened so his growled question came through gritted teeth. White-hot hatred burned in his eyes and pulsed in the air.

Maggie took a blinking step back before she got burned. *That* anger was aimed at the other cop? She'd hate to be a real enemy facing him.

"What did he say?" Harte repeated the question, each word a punishing punch.

"He answered your phone." She thought about ending there. "Apparently I don't know the pleasure I'm missing by preferring you to him because he can satisfy all my needs. Oh, and I have a name, but he seemed to be under the impression it was either sugar or darlin'. I felt the need for a shower when I hung up."

Harte's pupils shrank until the blue of his irises popped dominantly. He methodically clenched and unclenched his hands in tight fists while the veins in his neck bulged and throbbed. "I *will* deal with him."

"Let me know if you need a statement."

"The bastard would have an explanation."

She'd never witnessed a blind rage, yet didn't doubt for a second if Pritchett crossed Harte's path any time soon, Harte would find immense pleasure in making sure he was the closest thing to a dead man walking.

"He isn't worth killing," she murmured.

"Maybe not."

Mmm-mm-mm. She'd always gone for the brainy types, but the tightly leashed, raw power radiating from Harte, mixed with his spicy clove scent and downright sexiness called to her inner female. Seeing him at such a primal moment… Her pulse points pounded.

"Right." Maggie reached behind her and opened the door. A series of loud pops rang out. Wood splintered and stung her cheek.

She dove toward the floor. Her heart stampeded. Craig rushed outside in a semi crouch.

Harte seemed to materialize beside her, hovering so big she couldn't see beyond him as he stretched a leg out and kicked the door closed. The gun he hadn't been holding a moment ago pointed to the floor by his side.

"What was that?"

"I'm not sure." Harte cocked his head and focused on something she couldn't hear for a moment before easing her up and toward the couch. "Sit down."

Shaking her head, she pulled away and ran down the hall. Harte stopped pursuing her after two steps and a harsh curse.

He still stood cemented to the tile with pale cheeks and a terror-stricken stare when she returned from checking the kids. What had scared him *after* the fact? "Were those gunshots? Was someone shooting?"

"Maybe. It could be nothing."

It wasn't. He and Craig both knew it was something.

Worrying her wedding ring, she watched Harte shed the fear-filled shell and slip back into in cop mode. Alert. Brash. Utterly controlled and intense while he waited for Craig to return. She would have expected Harte to be the one seeking out danger while Craig soothed a woman's fears and worries.

"Mags?" Harte lowered his gun between his knees as he sat on the table in front of her. "Are you okay?"

She met his gaze and was struck by sincere warmth. Familiarity. He always called her Mrs. Sullivan. Until now. And she hated when people shortened her name, so why didn't it bother her with him? *Think about it later.* She took a deep breath and released it slowly. "Yes."

"You sure?" He leaned forward.

His blue eyes were gentle and wary, as if he expected her to wig out. Rooted in his gaze, arrested by his calm, she settled. Her pulse slowed to almost normal.

"Maybe." Instead of thinking of him as a grumpy detective who happened to be the star of her sex dreams, she saw him as a man who could be tender. A man who made her feel safe.

She looked around the room, took in the plastic covered paper now on the floor, the splinters of wood and the no longer unlocked windows.

A woman killed.

A gutted raccoon.

A picture of her late husband.

Getting shot at.

Everything was connected. Somehow. When she factored in Harte sleeping in his car outside of her home she became more certain. She wasn't safe.

"Mags?"

Their first instinct had been danger. And not entirely because they were used to it. Whatever had happened in the park had them on edge. And for the first time, she felt exposed and vulnerable in her home.

"I'm scared." She didn't like making the admission, especially to Harte. But she'd put it out there and couldn't rescind it now.

He rested a hand over hers. Sadness clouded his eyes when he met her gaze. "I'll take care of things."

"That doesn't change the facts." She thumbed her wedding ring in circles on her finger. Tingles from his touch were enveloping her right hand. "I'm afraid to take the kids to the park, I don't feel comfortable in my own house at night, and I can't shake the feeling someone's watching me—namely you."

His throat bobbed with a swallow. "I could come by more often...check in...sort of...be around."

He carried a gun and was big enough to make anyone think twice about breaking in. Not all bad. She'd just have to ignore the sizzle in her blood when he got close. Assuming she understood his proposal. "Are you suggesting you move in here?"

A cough sounded from the front door. Maggie jumped and turned her head. Harte jerked back. Craig stood, slack-jawed in the doorway for several "dun-dun-dun" singing seconds before shaking his cop mask back into place. "There are a few bullets in the door, but whoever was shooting is long gone or shot from a distance."

What was happening to her neighborhood?

She turned to Harte. "About you being around more..."

"You asked him to move in! You've got to be kidding!" Grace's eyes lit with mischief as she cradled Emma in her arms.

Grace was such a sweet sounding name for her sassy-mouthed meddling sister. In the year since Mike's death, they'd shifted from close sisters to best friends. Maggie had relied heavily on Grace's support during the pregnancy and the last few months of dealing with two children alone.

"I wish I were." Maggie rolled her eyes as she scrubbed at the blood on the front porch for the second time. She'd repaired the bullet holes in the doorframe last night. Grace only knew a woman had been found in the park and she thought the raccoon was a prank. Maggie omitted the bit about the paper. "I was…momentarily freaked."

Okay, she still was, but once she'd started telling Grace about Harte she'd quickly realized she needed to travel a different path if she was going to keep the gruesome truths from her pushy, though caringly so, sister.

Grace squatted in front of her and stilled. Worry pinched her flawless face. "What did he say?"

"Thanks, but no thanks. Worded more diplomatically." *Wouldn't want to hurt the victim's feelings.*

Maggie wiped the sweat from her forehead and kept scrubbing. Physical labor with the intention of releasing frustrations didn't work when she ended up talking about the source of the frustration.

"The idea was his to begin with, or I thought it was." She swiped at the sweat again and scrubbed harder. "He looked horrified at the prospect."

"Is it really the security of his presence you want?" Grace wiggled her brows. Her sister's spirit drew men in. Combine it with the smooth perfection of her Audrey Hepburn face and the fact she was financially well off and she became lethal.

"Please!" Maggie's system hadn't stopped revving until half an hour after Harte had left, but she wasn't telling Grace that. She had to focus on the protection. Prolonged exposure to the scrumptious detective could be troublesome. "He's upped the patrols in the neighborhood and has been spending the night in his car. He knows more than he's telling."

How is this not telling her too much? Shut up, Maggie.

Signs of joking slid from Grace's face as the ruling

concern and worry returned. "You're really scared."

"No. Curious." *I'm not sure even I buy that lie.*

"I could stay with you." Grace rubbed her nose against Emma's cheek. "You could bring the kids and stay with me."

"I know." Putting more muscle behind the scrubbing effort, Maggie avoided her sister's perceptive gaze and skill to see more than anyone was comfortable with. She'd known Grace would worry, which was why she'd left out any hint of a connection to the park. Getting Grace riled up would lead to her parents getting involved. She loved them all, knew they meant well, but she had to handle this on her terms.

Harte may be problematic, but he wouldn't insinuate himself in all the areas of her personal life. Plus, he was licensed to carry and shoot a gun. She would tell herself his staking her street out was enough. "Honestly, I'm fine."

"Maggie, I…"

A purring car engine drew their attention. They turned and watched the car roll slowly past.

"Isn't that Mike's old car?" Grace moved toward the edge of the porch.

"Yeah." The car he'd died in and that she thought had been destroyed. How had the wide-jawed, beefy man behind the wheel gotten it?

Shadowed by the angle of the sun, dark shades and a ball cap, she couldn't see the man's face as he tossed a padded envelope through the open passenger window onto her grass before speeding away. Spasms speared the muscles lining Maggie's spine.

The package looked harmless, but Maggie wasn't interested in finding another bloody gift. Or more pictures tying Mike to a dead woman, and she didn't want Grace seeing them either. She also wanted to figure out how the mystery driver had accessed Mike's car when the police had impounded it.

She grabbed Grace's leg when she started to move down the steps. "Leave it."

"I want to know what it is."

"Leave it." She pinned Grace with a glare and pulled out her cell to call Harte. He dispatched a patrol car to canvas the area for Mike's car and promised to be right over.

Maggie tried to get Grace to take the kids while she dealt with the cops, but her stubborn sister resisted until Harte and Craig pulled up less than five minutes later with a patrol car right behind them. Harte and Craig moved toward her and Grace. The officers headed to the envelope with some sort of scanner.

"Mrs. Sullivan." Craig addressed her, but his gaze lingered on Grace.

Grace handed Emma over to her and stepped toward Craig. "I would like to know what's going on around here."

Maggie stood behind Grace and shook her head at Craig begging him to watch his words. She was tired of being sheltered by her family, and it would only take knowing the raccoon wasn't a prank for them to close in.

"It looks like a prankster has zeroed in on your sister." Craig smiled lightly at Grace. "Why don't you come with me? Tell me what you noticed?"

"You're trying to hide something."

"Simply need to get your impressions without mixing them with Maggie's." Before Grace could argue, he took her elbow and led her away more smoothly than anyone had ever handled her sister.

Harte—with his gaze boring into Emma—stiffly closed the distance to Maggie. His hands worked in and out of fists at his sides. Emma rolled her head and blinked at him with the wide blue eyes she'd inherited from Mike's dad. Eyes nearly as blue as Harte's.

He ran his hands up and down his denim-clad thighs. His gaze never left Emma. "Whose baby?"

"Mine." She moved farther away from Grace to make sure her sister didn't get any worrisome details. "Emma's three months old. I was a few weeks pregnant when Mike died."

"Sh-she's gorgeous." His Adam's apple worked the words up in what sounded like a painful squeeze. He kept rubbing his thighs, his fingers clawing at his legs. Like he wanted to reach out, but was afraid.

"Thank you." She swayed slightly, side-to-side, and watched Harte.

His gaze flicked between her and Emma, lingering longer on Emma. He seemed uneasy in his own skin. And sad. "Harte."

Instead of saying more about Emma, he shifted visibly into cop mode with a hardening set to his jaw and shoulders. He asked her about the car and the person driving it. Not that she was able to give him much other than it being Mike's car, the man was big with a square jaw and he'd worn black glasses and a ball cap.

"Detective Harte?" The officers approached with the envelope.

"Yeah." He blinked and turned to Officers McClain and Lewis according to their nametags. "What's in the envelope?"

"An iPod." Officer McClain looked between her and Harte. Caution creased his face. "There's dried blood on it and an inscription on the back."

Lancing agony stabbed Maggie. She'd have clutched at her chest if Emma hadn't been in her arms. It couldn't be. It had to be.

"I wouldn't have missed the dance," she whispered.

The officers and Harte turned to her.

"It was Mike's last father's day gift. He had this thing for Garth Brooks and a few times the week before he died he'd quoted that line before going to work." It was the only thing that hadn't been returned to her after the wreck. It hadn't been in the car when the police searched it, so when had it been taken?

Tears she hadn't shed since Harte held her a year earlier built in her eyes.

"Maggie." Harte reached out.

She stepped back and swiped at her eyes before meeting his piercing gaze. *Focus on control.* "I'm fine. Grace knows about the woman in the park, but not her identity. She knows about the raccoon, but not the paper. I want to keep it that way."

He pointed toward her house. "There are gunshot holes in your door and a bloodstain on your porch. How are you going to hide those from her?"

"Thank you for the reminders." Her skin itched at the thought of the raccoon blood still lightly staining the porch. "I patched and painted the door frame. As far as she's concerned the raccoon was a kid's prank. I need her in the dark or my family will become…difficult."

Harte took the evidence bag the officers had slipped the envelope into. "After I have this processed I'll get it back to you."

"Thanks. Listen." She shifted Emma and looked over at Grace still talking to Craig. "This crap is really beginning to freak me out."

"I've upped patrols."

"And you're spending the nights in your car. Neither's helping me sleep and frankly, the neighbors are going to begin noticing things. Then *they'll* be freaking out."

"I—"

"Surely don't want everyone aware that you are on the lookout for…*something.*"

"Maggie."

She railroaded ahead. "You want to believe you'll do a better job of keeping an eye on things from your car. That it's enough to stop whatever you're expecting."

She shrugged and patted his arm. The brief touch was enough to register how big and hard his arms were and to make her wonder what it would be like to have them around her. Naked. *Not now!*

"The truth is, everything seems to be happening when you aren't around or watching. As if the person you suspect is watching closer than you."

"I could assign someone else."

"Like Detective Pritchett?"

His face hardened. Officer McClain stiffened and growled. Clearly Harte wasn't alone in his hatred. It was a low blow to mention him, but she had to make her point. She didn't trust her kids to *someone else*.

"The neighbors have seen you around." She nodded to the house across the street where an elderly couple watched from behind their blinds. "More cops will raise suspicions. If you intend to stake out my house again tonight, you may as well do it inside the air conditioning where there's a bathroom, food and fresh coffee."

He stood and stared and started to speak several times before finally saying, "I'll see you tonight," before he turned and headed over to his car.

Well, she'd won. Sort of. He would be in her home, around to disturb her mind on a constant basis. Perhaps it hadn't been the best plan and she may seriously regret it, but at least now she had a better shot at learning what he knew. And how it tied back to her or Mike.

She would just have to hope Jared didn't get too attached and, of course, be careful to avoid touching.

Chapter Three

"Sullivan should have helped. The wife will, or she'll meet the same end."

—Adalia

For two days following torment after torment culminating with the iPod toss, Adalia remained silent—probably to needle her way into Maggie's conscience and get her wondering. Worrying.

Mike's death hadn'tbeen an accident. Maggie's, if they failed to stop Adalia, wouldn't be anaccident. Figuring out how Mike had known Adalia, and who had tossed the iPod, would put them closer to puttin Adalia back behind bars.

An agreement to stay at Maggie's home became inevitable when she'd recited the inscription from the iPod. In that moment, remembering the man he'd met a year earlier as well as his regretful gaze, taking the song quote as a final message from Sullivan, BD knew why Mike had worried about her safety. With the acceptance came uncomfortable reality. There was no backing down and someone was going to get hurt.

He'd been back over and over the case files and still couldn't see the connection between victims. His gut, and ten years of police work, pointed to Mike as the key. How? How involved had Maggie's husband had been with Adalia? How did a linguistics professor with a gorgeous wife and kids in the suburbs get tangled up with a killer?

Shifting facts around in his mind, BD considered the background checks he'd run on Maggie and Mike. Rockewell-esque family history and solid financials, without any large deposits leading up to or following Mike's death aside from the life insurance payout. Thanks to a healthy policy and smart decisions, Maggie wouldn't have to worry about money, but BD had more to consider than her financial state.

Whatever Adalia wanted had to be money driven. Did

Maggie know about it? Did she have something without realizing it?

Things in the Sullivan house seemed fairly settled emotionally, but loss had a way of sneaking up, busting through egg-shell fragile memories and ripping new craters of grief in the heart. He worried he'd crack the shells if he worded a question wrong or came home when the kids were awake.

Not home. Can't think of it that way.

Even now, with the warning playing in his head as he sat in the circle driveway of her home, he couldn't stop wondering. Wanting.

He tried avoiding Maggie and the kids, staying close enough to protect yet distant enough to evade attachments. To her, her sad son, her blue-eyed daughter. The risk of attachment was huge for him. Maggie scared him, made him feel things, emotions, he'd long ago buried.

Time did not heal all wounds. Some experiences and losses cut too deep, until the slightest trigger rekindled a memory, good or bad. Like Emma with her breathtaking blue eyes. Jared with his wounded spirit trying to break free. Maggie caring for and playing with her kids.

Maggie.

She smiled sweetly, smelled heavenly and cared openly. Her brightness fractured his inner darkness and awakened the desire to touch her every time he got close. Too long in her company and he'd be a goner. This case needed to be solved fast, and that wasn't going to happen with him hiding in the car outside.

Renewed determination to do anything necessary to stop Adalia gripped him, propelled him out of the car and to the front porch.

Feeling like an intruder, even though Maggie had given him a key, BD stepped into the entryway and looked around her perfectly organized house. Earlier than normal, expecting some sort of chaos or drama, he instead heard silence.

Rather than set his bag of clothes in the entryway, he

carried it to the guest room to his left. She'd move it the first second she saw it anyway if he left it out. Any little thing that got nudged out of perfect alignment was quickly righted. Couch pillows sat a certain way, foods in the pantry were faced and categorized like in a grocery store. He didn't remember the house being quite so precise a year ago. Was her OCD a coping mechanism? A grasp for control?

Stepping back into the living room, he again noticed the quiet. Too quiet.

It wasn't a simple silence from no one being home or from everyone being asleep. There was more noise in the middle of the night. Now there was nothing. His neck tingled with a sudden chill of dread.

Unsnapping the safety on his holster and drawing his weapon, BD stepped down into the living room.

Adalia hasn't gotten to them.

He moved silently through the house, checking the office and bedrooms. Empty. His instincts hummed more with each room.

I didn't fail to protect her so quickly.

Hustling through the dining room, he heard an almost imperceptible clicking from the kitchen. With his gun lowered to his side he looked in.

Sitting cross-legged on the dining room table, pristinely dressed in pleated slacks and a satiny looking blouse, with her long hair neatly braided, Maggie focused on her laptop screen. Emma slept next to her in the carrier. A plastic tote tub with a garden hoe across the lid sat by a table leg.

Relief followed by curiosity rushed through him with a release of adrenaline. His muscles trembled as he reholstered his weapon. "What are you doing? Where's Jared?"

"Neighbor's." She chewed her lower lip. The skin flashed white, her jaw tightened. "If he stayed here I might have strangled him."

Another prank. BD resisted asking if the kid had smiled—the boy was eerily serious more often than not.

Asking meant caring. Caring meant involvement. Involvement meant danger.

The unconsciously erotic way she chewed on her lip, occasionally wetting it with her pink tongue, shot straight through BD. A pool of sweat formed at the base of his spine. The air conditioner made it impossible to blame the heat on anything other than arousal.

How would she taste? Would she quiver if he tried to find out?

Too late to dodge danger.

He licked his lips and blinked to break his stare and thought process. Maggie was built for long-term relationships while he chose short-term ones. Still, she appealed to him, disturbed him, threatened his focus. And he hadn't spent any real time with her.

He didn't do the damsel in distress, but twice now, she'd been cast in the role. Twice now he found himself turned on by the idea of saving her. *Twisted bastard.*

BD walked toward the table. Her radiating warmth and sensuality teased his senses and tempted him again to discover what she would be like when aroused. Curious to know how much exposure he could handle, just how long he'd last before his brain short circuited, he leaned in close and looked at the screen.

His body sizzled as if he'd grabbed hold of a live wire. Vanilla and rose scents floated around her, feminine and spicy. Arousing.

"Mags." He cleared his throat and looked at the snake on her screen. "I had no idea you were into snakes."

She freed her bottom lip, swollen from her own teeth. A drop of blood lingered where she'd bitten too hard. His tongue swiped across his own mouth, wishing it were hers. Sweat dripped along his spine. He should be focusing on the job. Not her.

"I'm not. Jared snuck one in."

He looked away from the image. He didn't have many

fears, but those icy, reptilian eyes made his skin crawl. "What kind?"

"Copperhead." She clicked a picture to enlarge it. Cold, black slits stared back at them.

"What? How… Those things are venomous."

"Apparently, he and his friend chased it into his backpack. I swear the kid's not going to the park for a month."

"Here? Copperheads don't live around here. Do they?"

"Not typically. I however seem to have one as a pet."

"You aren't keeping it." The panic in his voice irritated him even as he scanned the room and corners again, looking for any signs of the slithering, cold-blooded serpent.

She looked at him with a startled and suspiciously humored gaze. "Do I look like an idiot? Now, my neighbor across the street who's into fetishes might want it."

Okay, good to know she was mentally sound. And he'd heard about that neighbor from Craig after their door-to-door. No thanks. "How did they not get bitten?"

"He claims he propped the bag open with some sticks and put a dead rat in it." She shuddered. "I'm not thinking about how he zipped the bag without incident. Or unzipped it."

Thinking up the logistics of stunts like this before he hit ten? The kid was going to be trouble when he got older. He needed a new direction for his imagination. "Where did you find it?"

"It went under the couch."

"Where is it now?" BD looked around the room. No sign of it. A careful maneuver had him briefly brushing against her. Harmless. His system remained somewhat level.

Hmm. If he could be close to Maggie, maybe touch her while his nerves hummed with snake awareness, and stay in control then he could survive his stint in her home.

"Still there as far as I know."

It could be anywhere. Ready to strike. He could have walked right by it… No. He'd have noticed. Jared may be the culprit this time, but this was the kind of stunt Adalia would pull. Only she'd put the thing in the bed.

"I needed to verify the species before trying to catch it." She scooted over, presumably to give him more room, though he already had a foot of space on his other side and could easily have moved away from her.

Would she really just grab a snake like it was no big deal? Even non-venomous ones bit. And the bites hurt. BD pushed his shoulder blades back in an attempt to dislodge the shirt now stuck to the stream of sweat running along his spine.

"You know, the city employees people to handle these things. They're known as animal control."

"I grew up on a farm."

"So you've captured a copperhead before?" BD searched the floor again.

"No, but I *can* do this."

In other words she wouldn't back down from a challenge. He admired her even while he wished she'd leave the task to the professionals. He pointed to the tub and hoe.

"Now that you know what you're after, the kids are safe, and you seem prepared—" he couldn't believe what he was about to ask. She'd already rewired him somehow. "Do you want some help?"

"That would be great." She hopped off the table, handed him the hoe and picked up the tub. "You pin it. I'll handle the lid."

"Pin it and pick it up."

A wave of bile rushed into his throat. They were talking about catching a venomous snake and she seemed more excited that freaked. Something had to crack her elaborate mask of control.

They headed toward the living room with her slightly behind him. "You think it's still under the couch?"

"Your guess is as good as mine." Not certain how best to approach a confirmation, he sure as hell wasn't sticking his face down there, he edged toward the back of the sofa. "Get behind me."

Once she'd done as he said, he backed them both up. Hoping they were out of striking range, he used the hoe to lift the fabric skirt at the bottom of the sofa and bent at the waist.

Nothing, not even a dust bunny was under the couch. A slight scuffling came from behind the entertainment center. He straightened and watched the snake slither from behind the massive piece of woodwork. A long, shiny, white-tipped, red tongue followed by a copper-colored head and a long body slid around the wall toward the bedrooms.

"They seem so harmless from a distance," she mused.

BD turned his head. Slowly. *Gorgeous. Brave. And off her rocker.*

"It's headed to my room." She moved past him. Her curvy hip brushed against him. A blast of heat shot through him instantly awakening his body.

He blocked her, not caring if she noticed his arousal. Maybe she'd be shaken to know he'd pictured her in bed. It was certainly a more appealing image than the current activity. "Doesn't anything rattle you?"

"No." She stepped aside to circle around him.

"That's not possible."

"It is."

"Bullshit." No one could be so cool all the time and, snake be damned, he'd prove it.

BD grabbed her arm and yanked her around. She dropped the bin. He dropped the hoe, pulled her against him and kissed her honey and cinnamon flavored, plump lips. His blood surged.

If she'd only open up.

Stepping closer, needing to feel more of her, to be closer to the fire, he picked her up and sat her on the back of the sofa. He stood between her thighs and wrapped his arms around her. Her satin blouse slid against his palms as soft as what he imagined her skin would be when he got the chance to touch her. Sinking deep into her, his mouth playing over hers, he enticed her to open.

Scents of hot summer, vanilla and roses engulfed him. Maggie dug her blunt fingernails into his shoulders, clinging. The heat in his veins raged like a blue flame begging for more fuel.

He pressed against her, molding himself to her pliant curves that fit him like heavenly sin. He moaned as his tongue swept across her slightly parted lips, seeking an entry he wasn't sure she would give.

She did.

She opened her mouth and invited him in as a quiver racked her body.

Triumph echoed in his chest. Breathing grew difficult within his shrinking ribcage. She wrapped her legs around his waist and pressed against his erection. Tingles spread along the top of his scalp.

"I want you. Here. Now."

Her quiver turned into tremors racking her body. More than arousal drove her. *Fear?* BD raised his head. Her eyes were wide, her breath was ragged and her fingers shook as she hung onto him.

Never should have kissed her.

He'd rattled her and himself. He knew her taste, her feel, her smell. He'd never forget them and he wanted them again even while telling himself a repeat was too pricey.

"That was a mistake." BD stepped back and set her on her feet. Unable to look at her flushed cheeks, or name the look in her eyes, he picked up the hoe and slowly moved toward the hallway.

Idiot. Stick to safe women. No more thoughts of getting Maggie naked.

Catch the snake. Re-establish a professional distance. Repeating the orders in his head, he stepped into her room. *Don't look at the bed or think of her in it.*

She came in behind him. Their prey was coiled in a corner. Perfect striking position.

Maggie set the bin down and peered around BD. Her lush

breast brushed lightly against his arm. The erection straining against his zipper throbbed.

"It's huge," she whispered.

The snake. She means the snake. BD rolled his eyes to the ceiling. Stupid kiss had his mind too far south. "He's not that big."

Maggie's nearness, the feel of her body, the sight of her bed less than five feet away couldn't matter. Catching the snake mattered.

And it *was* big. Easily as big around as his forearm, longer than his leg, and it liked to eat things. BD tightened his stomach muscles against the urge to turn away. Being as still as possible, he called on his training and calmed his racing heart.

He hated snakes. The way their fangs sank through flesh. The venom spreading through the body. It only took one bad move as a kid to get struck. His wrong move had landed him in a hospital at the age of five.

"You don't think that's big?" Maggie's hushed question brushed his arm.

"Mags, honey, I think you're scared of him." He tsked her playfully. "And you say you grew up on a farm."

"Cautious. A lesson learned well on that farm."

He took her hand and squeezed. "It'll be fine. He's not going to bite us."

"He? How do you know it's a him?" Her chin still angled over his shoulder. All he had to do to taste her again was lean left a tad and... BD mentally slapped himself.

"Why else would he head to a beautiful woman's bedroom?"

"Harte!"

"Now I know I'm in trouble." He turned his head and met her gaze. "You've employed the mom tone."

"You may think this is funny. I don't." She pushed up on her feet until her nose almost bumped his. She was too small to reach him unless he stooped down. "Catch that damn thing."

Ooh, the lovely lady cussed. She *was* rattled. "Open the

tub."

She pulled the green tub closer, and then stepped around it so the lid formed a shield. Amazing. She didn't look ridiculous with her legs braced wide as she prepared to catch a venomous snake while dressed like she was going to an afternoon tea.

BD spread his legs and raised his hands, one with the hoe, the other formed in a fist. His pulse thundered in his ears. He caught his reflection in the mirror and groaned inwardly. He looked like he was preparing to attack some crazed maniac, which was his preference. "Okay, babe. Here we go."

Taking a deep breath, he reached toward the snake's head with the hoe. When his arm shook, he hesitated. He'd lost his mind. They should've grabbed Emma and left this to Animal Control. Saying so now would make him look weak.

Willing himself to remain steady, he stretched out the hoe and jammed the flat blade down, pressing the snake's head into the floor. His hand shook. The snake wriggled its body. Stepping gently on the blade, not wanting to squish brain matter all over the carpet, he made sure the head and mouth were well secured. He closed his eyes and counted to five in another attempt to slow his heart rate.

Bending, he grabbed the wriggling copperhead just behind its head in a tight grip. No matter how much his palms sweated, he wasn't losing his grip. Removing his foot from the hoe blade, he let it fall to the floor as he took the weight of the struggling reptile in his hands.

He stepped over to the empty tote, and lowered the tail in. If he thought he could do it without drawing attention he'd take the tote outside when they finished and fill it with bullets. It would be a Catholic cleanse.

"All right, Mags."

"Don't lose your grip." She moved closer, positioning the lid over the box, leaving him room to drop in the snake and jerk his hand free.

"Not an option." Its mouth hung open above the fists of his sweat-slicked hands. Soulless eyes met his. "Okay. On three."

"Like one, two, three then drop or drop on three."

He breathed deep and swallowed. "Drop on three."

"Got it." Maggie held the lid in both hands, legs braced apart and completely ready. "Move fast."

"Right." No big deal. People moved faster than pissed off, venomous snakes every day. He held her gaze and nodded.

"One…" Adrenaline zinged through his system. "Two…" He was a goner if their timing was off. "Three."

BD dropped the snake. Its body plopped into the base of the tub. Maggie slammed the lid down. He pressed his foot on the lid to make sure it stayed shut.

"Don't move. I'll be right back." She ran from the room, leaving him alone with the snake and no clue what she was doing.

Adrenaline surged, expanded his veins until the heated blood itched his skin. He took advantage of her absence and indulged in a furious torso scratch to banish the pervasive itch. It helped a little.

She returned with a bungee cord and hooked the ends of it to each handle of the tote to make sure the lid stayed secure.

"Copperheads hang out in packs," he said, proud of how calm he sounded. "I'll call Animal Control. Let them know there may be more of these things around."

"Right." Maggie stepped over to him, wrapped her hands around his neck, pulled him down, and kissed him long and sweet. "Thank you."

When she pulled back, he wound an arm around her waist and pulled her tight against him. He'd be sorry later. Bending down, he devoured her mouth. Releasing all the adrenaline and energy zipping through his blood was impossible, but the outlet of her honey-flavored mouth was a beginning.

She trembled. He deepened the kiss, sweeping his tongue along hers. Sliding his hands down her curves, past the sexy indention of her waist and over her hips he pulled her closer. A rumble rose up in his chest. He ached to pull her to the king bed with the fluffy duvet and pillows.

She pushed her hand against him and pulled her head back.

Reluctantly, he let her go and cleared his throat. The first kiss had been impulse fueled by the desire to know her taste. The last one had been greed sentencing him to want more. More than he could have.

He was here to work, gain insights into her husband and their life together. Even facing his worst childhood memory hadn't been as awful as kissing Maggie.

Chapter Four

Maggie had watched Harte carry in boxes and dodged Grace as long as possible. She'd asked him to make the move *official* after Jared had come home asking questions about her new bed buddy. Though she'd explained to Jared he was not allowed to say such things, she hadn't been able to explain why Harte was around.

Having him move his things in made the arrangement seem less temporary. Less clandestine. She promised herself it only mattered for image's sake with the neighbors. He would be leaving. It didn't matter that his kisses thrilled her and kept her awake at night. She was not, as Grace suggested, interested in more.

A relationship would force open the door she'd firmly locked. Moving on with her daily life was one thing. But with a man? No. No matter how sexy he may be, or how his voice made her skin tingle as if he'd whispered a favorite endearment against her ear. A promise of forever was too fragile, so she'd stick to things she could control. Her heart would be counted on that list.

"I'm going to make some drinks." Maggie pushed off the floor and tossed a burp cloth to Grace. "Can you watch Emma and keep Jared out of trouble?"

"Sure."

In the kitchen, away from Grace's probing eyes, she stood at the sink and tried to focus on something other than Harte. Something other than the feel of his touch, his commanding lips, the flare of heat still coursing through her from days earlier.

She stared into the backyard with dark clouds off in the distance. The threatening rain would be vengeful when it hit, and would do little to cool the record temperatures engulfing Dallas. She'd have to check the flashlight batteries. Storms always knocked out her power.

The bushes that had gotten out of control over the last year would explode after a solid soaking. Pity. She hated those bushes and their rigid box cut.

"Hmm." The bushes were one more thing she'd let Mike dictate.

Maggie slumped against the counter. Mike had been a good man. A great man she'd loved. She just didn't love who she'd become with him. Her feelings had been set aside for the sake of keeping the peace and her escape had been the dreamy world of romance novels while she coped with reality.

Going along with him, like on so many other things, had been so easy she'd never noticed it bothering her or how often she'd kept her opposing opinion to herself. She'd been so wrapped up in pleasing him she'd lost herself, and if she allowed Grace to psychoanalyze her, she suspected her sister would say she was still lost.

Harte reminded her of Mike because of his differences and made her wonder if fiction heroes were based partly on reality. Maybe some men thrived on the emotional connections and truly valued their life partners.

Staring at the bushes, those boring ass bushes with nothing special about them, she shook her head. She'd shoved the loss, the pain, the coldness of being alone down, took care of her children and told herself she was happy. She controlled every aspect of her life, minus her own emotions and happiness. The bushes, the neighborhood drama, Harte's presence... They all had her wondering. Doubting.

"I hate you," she addressed the bushes.

Mike had claimed their constancy reminded him of her. She now saw their lack of color and originality as a mirror of her relationship with him. "It's my fault. I never told him."

Gripping the counter edge, she tilted her head and pictured the yard as she'd wanted it. With a lattice and climbing roses of varying colors and personality. Thorns. She'd had too much perfection, structure and predictability. She wanted something a little wild. Hard to tame.

Maggie rolled her shoulders back and called into the living room. "Grace, I'm going outside."

Determined to live life her way, she went to the garage and grabbed a pair of hedge clippers. She hit the button to raise the garage door and tapped her foot. Waiting. Those bushes were coming out.

Now.

Opening the gate, she marched across the yard and started whacking away at the closest bush. Each branch she chopped off filled her with pleasure and satisfaction. Freedom and independence she'd long forgotten soaked into her with renewed dreams and opinions. She was more than a mom and homemaker.

"Mags, what are you doing?"

She looked over her shoulder. Harte stood just inside the iron gate. Craig leaned against the truck behind him waiting to move the workout equipment and more boxes in the garage. "If you can't see the obvious, then you can't be a very good detective."

"Looks like you're cutting the bushes."

"You get a gold star for observation skills."

Craig smothered a laugh behind twitching lips.

"Why now?" Harte glanced briefly back at his partner before turning his attention back to her. "What did they do to you?"

"Existed." She hacked another branch. And then three more. Harte silently went back to help Craig unload the truck.

Did all men think bushes needed to be plain, boring green? Did they all have a problem with a woman having a mind of her own? With her wanting a little color in her yard? So what if wisteria and rose bushes had to be trimmed back more often. They were pretty. They smelled nice.

Using her foot to push a branch to the ground, she leaned forward and put the cutters at the base. Squeezing the handles together so hard every muscle in her arms screamed their protest, she worked at cutting the damn thing off.

Crack!

It broke with a snap. Her foot slipped off the branch. She lost her balance and fell into the bushes.

The freshly cut limbs sliced at her arms. The newest cut one jabbed into her knee, ripping her new slacks, and scraping off a thick layer of skin.

"Shoot."

She threw the cutters to the ground and stormed into the house. Marching through the living room she headed for her room to clean her knee and change.

"Maggie, is—"

"Not now, Grace." Ignoring her sister currently pacing the floor with Emma, she stepped into the dimly lit hall. A movement to her right had her turning as a tall, slender woman wearing sunglasses stepped out of the office at the other end of the hall.

The woman stopped and grinned. "Enjoy Detective Harte while you can." With the cryptic message, she headed for the front door.

Chills skittered along Maggie's neck. She'd heard that voice. Seen that woman. Following, she tried to figure out where. And what she was doing in the house.

By the time Maggie reached the end of the hall and turned the corner, the woman was outside and half way across the lawn. Maggie looked toward Grace. "Who was that?"

"I don't know. Maybe Jared or one of the guys let her in while I was changing Emma." Grace cradled Emma in one arm and ran her finger along Emma's gums. "Is it too early for her to be teething?"

"Not really." Unable to worry about her daughter's possible tooth at the moment, she turned back to the open door. The woman was heading across the street a few houses down.

Shadows of dread weighed Maggie down as she stepped out on the porch. The woman got into a car and slowly pulled away from the curb, slid her glasses up onto her head and looked right at Maggie. Her cold stare was an invisible dagger to the heart.

She'd felt the chill of that stare.

Son of a...

Shivers swarmed. Maggie. She pivoted and ran toward the garage. Toward Harte.

BD sat some weights on the rack they'd just finished putting back together as Maggie stepped into the garage with fire in her eyes and a limping step. Her perfectly pleated, tan slacks were torn and bloody around the knee, her arms were scratched up and her hair had fallen out her braid.

Instantly he moved toward her. "What happened?"

"Jared, inside with Grace." The line of her jaw hardened beneath the stress of sounding calm for her son.

"But, Mom—"

"Now." The command stretched between clenched teeth and glared at BD.

"Jare." He laid his hand on the boy's shoulder. Rage radiated around Maggie, but she somehow retained a cool façade of control. His gut clenched, but he maintained a level voice for Jared. "We won't finish without you."

Maggie closed the door behind her son and glared. "Answers. Now."

Craig mumbled something about the truck and vanished.

She knew something, but BD wasn't saying anything without more information. "Excuse me."

"There is no excuse for you." She grabbed a twenty-pound weight and plopped it on the rack with a clang like it weighed nothing. "I want answers about Adalia Wood."

Shit. What did she know? "She went to prison a year ago."

Maggie picked up another weight and sat it on the rack. He resisted the urge to step back from her.

"What is she doing in my home?"

The gun nestled at his back grew heavy. She couldn't

know Adalia had targeted her, that Mike's murderer was out, which complicated the need to keep his investigation secret. It was a complication they didn't need. "How can you be sure it was Adalia?"

"I remember the face of the woman responsible for my husband's death. Why, the day you move in, does she come into my home? Is she behind the murder in the park? The raccoon? The iPod? Is she why you're really here?"

"Craig!" His blood chilled. She was too close to putting it all together, but worse was Adalia's willingness to make her taunts so blatant. "I need details, Maggie."

"Adalia Wood, who crashed into my husband's car after killing several people, just walked out my front door and drove away."

"Craig!" He yelled again and edged Maggie toward the kitchen door. "What kind of car?"

"Late-model, four-door Honda Accord. Dark blue." She crossed her arms and recapped what had happened. "She's gone."

Craig came into the garage with the hedge clippers in hand. "Yeah?"

"Adalia was here." Knowing his partner would catch up to them after calling for a patrol of the area, he relayed the necessary intel Craig needed to issue an all points bulletin.

Craig headed into the kitchen with his phone already to his ear. He would run interference with Grace and Jared to minimize the disturbance of any evidence. BD moved to the wall with the garage door button to lower the door. Adalia may still be in the area, and he wasn't about to make it easy for her to get in a second time.

"When did she get out of prison? Why is she in *my* house?" Maggie lowered her voice as they stepped in the kitchen. Her jaw muscles ticked. "What is going on? What have you brought to my home?"

He hadn't brought Adalia here. Adalia brought him. "Come with me."

Grabbing Maggie's elbow, he escorted her into the living room. She'd asked him to make her feel safe. He wasn't off to a great start, but neither had he thought Adalia would walk in the front door of a crowded house. He wouldn't underestimate her again.

"What's going on?" Grace asked.

Ignoring her, he met Maggie's gaze. "Stay here. Open the door for no one."

He turned to go to the office. She was on his heels. "Harte."

Lowering his voice to keep Jared and Grace from hearing, he shook his head. "You wanted me here. Stay out of my way."

She swiped her tongue over her teeth in a slight sucking sound and turned back toward the living room. He'd witnessed an inner strength beneath her fancy clothes, but now it threatened to be trouble. He admired her for her even as he wished it away. Her go-with-the-flow temperament had been replaced with a new independence.

He went into the office with Craig and closed and locked the door.

"Patrols are scouting the area." Craig reached into a box they'd brought in earlier and pulled out some latex gloves. He tossed a pair to BD.

"She'll be gone." BD caught the gloves and snapped them on. Shoving back his rage so he could concentrate on the investigation, he noticed nothing appeared to be out of place except his piles of boxes, but she'd had a reason for being there. "She wouldn't have shown herself to Maggie without being confident she'd get away."

"You shouldn't take it out on Maggie." Craig sifted through the papers beside a comfortable looking armchair. "She came to you instead of trying to follow Adalia."

"After following her outside… She could've been hurt." Adalia had been too close. "What was Adalia looking for?"

"Nothing seems to have been messed with. And why wait until we're both here to come in?"

"Power."

Helplessness was an unfamiliar feeling, but it was how BD felt at the moment. "Maggie is a stay-at-home mom. She shouldn't be on Adalia's radar."

"It goes back to the husband. It has to."

Adalia wouldn't have had much time. Craig looked through the numerous books on the shelves. BD opened the top drawer of Maggie's desk to discover tidily organized pens, pencils, paperclips, staples, rubber bands, scissors, a small tube of hand lotion and a lip gloss. The second drawer was filled with color-coded and alphabetized files he pushed backward and forward. Finding nothing behind, between or under the files he flipped through each one.

"If these were pleasure reads, Sullivan must've been a blast." Craig placed a book back on the shelf and pulled out another one.

"Why?"

"Most of them make school textbooks look exciting, or are written in bizarre languages and symbols."

"He was a linguist with a specialty in ancient languages." And yes, it sounded boring.

"Whatever." Craig continued looking for anything Adalia left behind.

She always left something behind.

"Why come straight in here?" Going through Maggie's bills and personal documents was an invasion of her privacy necessity did nothing to minimize. She had never been just a part of the job and deserved better than this. He shifted to another file. "It wouldn't have taken long to plant something or look for something obvious to her. She had to know the house layout to target this room. How?"

"City Planning office would have blueprints, or she's been watching the place close enough to know the layout." Craig placed a book on the shelf and turned. "I'm finding nothing."

"Keep looking. At the very least we'll find a note."

"She would have put it someplace obvious."

"Obvious to us or to Mags?" Sitting back in the chair, BD looked around the warm and welcoming room with a great view of the street through a large grouping of windows. Walking to the window he turned. With the blinds mostly open, it wouldn't be hard to know what was in the room. "To brave coming in here she would have had a plan. Precise timing."

"Makes sense." Craig sat another book back on the shelf.

"She's been watching, but she has help." The mystery there was who?

"She thought this room was the best place to find whatever she's after."

"She plays games, but is methodical with them." Viewing the room the way Adalia would have seen it from outside, BD considered the options.

Discounting the bookshelves and the table by the reading chair, the desk would've been the obvious choice. She wanted her message to be received, but she'd want to control who found it—Maggie.

Returning to the desk, BD sat and picked up the mail in an envelope sorter. Flipping through the envelopes, he found a paper folded neatly between two bills with Maggie's name scrawled on the outside.

"Found something."

Craig approached as BD opened the letter.

"The cops will not get in the middle again. I'll have the key to harnessing the power."
   —Adalia

What had they gotten in the middle of, other than a killing spree? What kind of power did she think she could harness?

"Maybe she went a little insane on the inside." Craig sat on the corner of the desk.

"What kind of key harnesses power? Is she talking magic or something more tangible?"

Craig grabbed a pencil and began flipping it between his

fingers. "You buy into magic?"

"No, but if it means stopping Adalia I'll explore it." He rolled his shoulders back. Maggie was a room away and he felt her breathing down his neck. "I have to end this fast."

"Right." Craig hesitated. The pencil never slowed down. "Is there anything in her old notes?"

BD shoved out of the chair to pace. He couldn't dodge the impotence of having his hands tied. "I'm not seeing any connections."

He had a promise to keep to Mike Sullivan and a family to protect, a deranged killer to put back behind bars and a strong desire to taste the forbidden to ignore. The promise and the desire for Maggie proved the most difficult. In ten years on the job, he'd never blurred the line of involvement. Craig the Tender Heart took the lead when someone needed sympathy, but with Maggie... The lines were more than blurring. They were vanishing.

Samantha's death hadn't been as grizzly as Sullivan's, but her face had flashed in BD's mind as he'd sat with Maggie's husband. Then he'd followed Maggie to her bathroom, held her while she threw up and comforted her while she wept.

One glance and she awakened everything he had sworn to never feel again. A year of distance had changed nothing. Her grief brought his back. Her family made him remember all he had once wanted.

Her voice, slightly breathless, sometimes skimmed over his skin in a feather-soft stroke. Samantha had sounded the same at the end. Even as she'd said it wasn't his fault, his heart ripped to shreds.

In every obvious way, Maggie was nothing like Sam. She preferred things orderly. Her understated sensuality hid beneath tailored slacks and silky tops. Sam had been messy and blatantly sexy with a preference for low-rise jeans and snug T-shirts with outrageous sayings.

"Do you think Maggie would know what key Adalia's talking about?"

"I don't know." BD pinched the bridge of his nose and forced his thoughts back to the case. He could worry about Maggie's appeal and Sam's fading memory later. Much later. "Right now she thinks Adalia's here because of me. If I ask her about this, she's going to put things together."

"Assuming she hasn't already."

A possibility he couldn't ignore.

"How are you going to handle this?"

"No clue." She would be well armed with questions by now and she'd be relentless if he didn't have a great explanation. "What are the chances Sullivan was having an affair with Adalia?"

"It doesn't seem likely from his file." Craig waved his hands at the room. "Look around this place. The man was a straight arrow. Dull."

BD's stomach knotted. "Unless he was leading a double life."

"Man, you can't let her know that's crawling around in your head."

"And I was thinking of leading with it." Without proof the supposition would only crush her. He pulled a blank envelope from her desk, slipped the note inside and handed it to Craig. "Take care of this and keep Grace and the kids out of the way." He turned to the door preferring an old fashioned firing squad or a stoning. "I'll talk to Maggie."

"I'm getting the better deal."

They stepped out of the office into silence like the one from the other night.

Something was wrong.

Adrenaline flooded his veins. If he found her in danger, he'd take out the offender. If he found her safe... *She better hope she's in danger*. He couldn't protect a woman incapable of following orders and staying put.

Years of training had his blood slowing as he went on the defensive. Adalia had not gotten in again so fast. They pulled their guns. He went right toward the bedrooms. Craig headed left through the entry toward the guest room and dining room. They met in the living room and shook their heads. Empty.

The kitchen was empty too. *Where are they?*

"Grace's car is still out front."

Half way across the kitchen to check the garage, he heard a grunt and a thwack. The hair on his neck quivered. He wanted to run across the room, jerk open the door and barge in. Training had him waiting for Craig. Standing to the side, he twisted the knob. Craig stooped down to go low.

After a brief nod, they went through the door together.

Chapter Five

Maggie shifted her weight and studied her opponent. Taking her time to calculate the most effective attack, she crouched, sprang and delivered a hard side kick. The punching bag wobbled creakily in the brackets.

Who did Harte think he was? Lying to her about his presence, letting her think he was doing her a favor. Pretending he hadn't known Adalia Wood was out of jail. Ordering her around. Locking doors on her.

He wasn't getting away with it.

Landing lightly on her feet, she eyeballed the bag. Her knee ached, a little swollen from the branch incident, but she was glad she'd changed clothes and sent the kids with Grace. Sitting around the living room would've driven her batty.

The woman who'd killed four people, including Mike, was back. She couldn't change it. She couldn't accept it without question. The state should've bumped up their schedule on the lethal injection. They should have informed her of the release.

Bouncing side to side on the balls of her feet, she delivered alternating punches into the imaginary images of Adalia Wood and Harte rotating over the bag. They were both playing mind games with her. Both were doomed to failure.

"Sweet hell." Harte's voice startled her.

She spun and looked into his aroused blue eyes. "Go away."

"Mags, where are Grace and the kids?"

"I preferred not to have witnesses when I sliced off your balls and roasted them for dinner."

"Well," Craig cleared his throat and backed toward the kitchen. "On that note, I'll go take care of…stuff."

Narrowing her eyes she watched Harte's partner. "Chicken."

"Smart." He smiled as he slapped Harte on the back hard

enough to propel him three steps forward. "I'm not the one on the chopping block."

Turning to Harte, she waited eager to see if he led with the truth or excuses.

"I told you to stay in the living room."

"I'm a grown woman. This is my house. I chose not to."

Shrugging, she turned back to the bag and hit it again with a little less force. Twenty minutes of punishing hits and kicks had her muscles burning. If she went much longer at that rate she wouldn't be able to move for three days.

"Next time, do what I say." He walked to the opposite side of the bag. "The empty house worried me."

"Awww. I might almost think you gave a jackelope's ass." She slid her eyes back to the bag before punching it hard enough to have the ceiling and floor brackets rattling. "Except they aren't real and you're lying."

"Mags."

Punch. "Harte, if you 'Mags' me one more time I'm going to use your face instead of this bag."

Punch.

He cleared his throat. "Maggie, I have a job to do. This may be your home, but there are things I'm not at liberty to discuss."

He paced the width of the garage like a caged animal. The rage pulsing from him was so thick her sharpest kitchen knife wouldn't penetrate it. Watching him hold it in was amazing, but didn't change things.

She had a brain. He'd known who had targeted her or he would have held to his resolve to not move in.

Conflicted between worry and anger, suddenly too exhausted to land another punch, she bit a strip of Velcro with her teeth to pull off a glove. After removing the second one, she stretched lightly to keep her muscles from tightening up.

She wasn't invisible, boring or willing to be pushed around. He had another think coming if he thought he could issue orders and expect her to blindly follow. Whatever kind of women he was used to being around, she wasn't one of them.

Her privacy had been invaded and Harte had reverted to caveman mode. With the sensation of a hundred fuzzy spiders running across her exposed skin, impressions of dirty filth suffused her. She had never felt more violated and scared in her life. More betrayed.

The haven she had designed for her children, their security and peace of mind, had been threatened. If Adalia had marched into her living room and held a gun to her head, she could have handled it better.

"You will answer my questions." *Or get out.* "I'm not playing mind games with you on top of everything else."

Blowing out a deep breath, she assured herself she could and would remain calm, rational and logical. She would not become irrational. Well, any more so than she already had.

Narrowing her eyes, she studied him and again waited. Instead of cool caution, his stare remained glacial. Every muscle in his giant body was taut. His jaw twitched. The bulging vein in his neck throbbed. He fisted and un-fisted his hands. She'd done the same things before working the bag.

Menace vibrated off him and grabbed her by the throat. His nostrils flared slightly with each breath. As surely as she knew he wouldn't tell her everything, she knew he itched to pound the stuffing out of something. Impatience warred with logic. She wanted answers, but she may have better luck if she let him cool off.

She walked to the cabinet in the wall that hid the punching bag when she released it from the floor and ceiling anchors, pulled out a larger pair of boxing gloves, and tossed them to him. A feral grin spread across his face as he secured the Velcro fasteners.

She stepped back and sat on his weight bench. Once his hackles lowered she would demand answers. Or maybe she'd take advantage of the distraction the bag provided.

Like the caged beast had been set free, he went after the bag. His fists hammered the leather, bouncing the bag a little.

The echo of his power and satisfaction sang in her body. She'd spent many sleepless nights in the garage with only the bag for company.

With each slap of leather against leather, Harte's wrath mounted rather than eased. Rolling his shoulders back, he pummeled the bag. For five minutes the sounds of his rough breathing and leather slapping the bag dominated the garage.

He became the distraction. Maggie leaned back against the barbell and extended her legs on the bench with her ankles crossed.

His muscles coiled and released beneath the power of each precisely delivered blow. He worked out with punching bags often. Her brain flashed to an image of him working out shirtless and her breath stuttered.

Don't go there. She shook her head clear. "How long have you known Adalia was out?"

"Since the first morning I came here." He pivoted his hip to put more power behind the punch. The mounting brackets clanged.

"Why wasn't I notified of her release?"

The dangerous edge of his temper surged briefly. His shoulders jerked. His hands fell to his sides and he stared at the bag with his chest heaving. "She wasn't released."

Maggie leaned forward, not sure she'd heard him correctly. He'd spoken so quietly. "Excuse me?"

"She escaped."

Swarmed with building heat, she gritted her teeth. "The woman killed my husband. Shouldn't I have been told?"

He sighed and turned to her. Anguish deepened the laugh lines around his eyes. "It wasn't my decision."

No apologies. No evasions. No explanations. How was she supposed to argue with a man who wouldn't argue?

Instead, he stood before her with sweat soaking his hair and running down his temples. His T-shirt clung tightly to his chiseled torso and had her thinking more about the masterful sculpture that was his body. She'd love to explore him, to again feel the press of him against her.

She bit into her lower lip. Sweaty men had never done it for her. Harte did. The leashed power he'd only partially shown as he ripped into the bag amazed her. Aroused her when she shouldn't be aroused.

Focus! She swung her legs off the bench and went to Harte. Struggling to organize her thoughts, she took the gloves he'd removed and carried them to the storage cabinet. His spicy and masculine scent trailed her. Awareness fluttered in her gut. "I need answers."

She hadn't been afraid of him when he'd looked ready to murder, but now, with raw energy pulsing off him, he threatened her. She craved him. His passion. His ability to make her forget her own name with a brief kiss. Adalia wasn't the only thing she needed answers about, but she was priority.

He said nothing. Maggie turned back to see him on the floor inspecting the bar extending out the base of the bag. When he stood, he looked at the ceiling, grinning.

Now that's power.

His pleasure with the bag filled her with pleasure. She liked that he'd found something in her home that pleased him. Too much of that pleasure was detrimental to her safety.

"This is genius. Who did it?"

"Me."

His head jerked to her in shock. "You?"

"Yes." He could have sounded a little less archaic in his shock. "You see, we little women aren't helpless. We don't need chauvinistic men around to do things for us, tell us what to think, or when to move."

"I never said you were helpless." He wrinkled his brow and slid his gaze down her body before slowly working his way back up. "And I'm not a chauvinist."

"Great. Then behave as if you believe that." His survey of her body had her blood sizzling…not entirely from anger. "Why wasn't I told Adalia was out? Why is she here?"

"I don't have those answers."

She crossed her arms over her chest, braced her legs apart. She'd wanted to be calm and rational. Too bad. "Harte—"

"Mags—" He stepped forward with a hand out. "Maggie, can't you trust me on this?"

"I could ask the same of you. Things were sane until you showed up. But now a woman has been killed, I've dealt with one screwed up prank after another, and my husband's killer has been in my home. You give me no answers, but want me to trust you."

"It would be easier."

"For you." Unable to stand still and unwilling to pace nervously, she moved to the punching bag. Bending down, she slid the pole from the floor up into the base of the bag. "You should have warned me."

"I couldn't."

She opened her mouth and then shut it. Disbelief gripped her throat. "You're trying to decide if I'm somehow involved. Do you think I as somehow responsible for Mike being there that day?"

"No." His pinched expression belied the adamant tone as he raked his hand through his hair. "But we didn't want to alarm you in the event nothing more happened."

"You're days too late." After securing the hook to hold the pole in the base of the bag, she grabbed the bag with both hands, twisted it counter-clockwise to release it from the locked position in the ceiling and then shoved it along its track to the cabinet in the wall. "*That's* why you agreed to move in here."

"My not wanting to be here had nothing to do with you."

"Sure. Every girl knows that really means it has everything to do with her." With nothing else to do, she went and sat on the end of his weight bench. "You make believing you impossible."

His shoulders dropped as he walked over and knelt in front of her. "My captain, when I briefed him, ordered me not to tell you what's going on."

Arguments and demands danced on her tongue. She chose a different route. "Are my kids in danger? Is Adalia going to come into my house again? You're a cop. What the hell are you doing to stop her?"

"It's not that easy, Mags."

Knowing he was right didn't settle her. She'd been holding things in, going along, for too long. His dismissal busted through her reserve and allowed all the pressure to escape. "It's plenty easy. I want to know what you know. Why you thought I needed to be watched. What does she want?"

"I don't have answers for you."

Arrgh. The man could be dense and she was losing her patience in the glare of his omissions. "You knew she was out. You should have stopped it. None of this should have happened."

His head jerked back as if she'd struck him. She didn't care.

"You could have *asked* me to stay in the living room. You could have taken one minute to act civil rather than acting like a know-it-all jerk ordering me around. Rather than acting like Detective Pritchett."

He worked his mouth like he was going to say something. She stayed still and shook her head. If he left, he could take Adalia with him. "You being here is a mistake."

"Too late. You said yourself I made you feel safer." Harte stood, towering over her as he shook his head. "Guess what, sweetheart. I was doing my job in the living room. I don't have time for niceties and patting you on the head like a little kid when there's danger or a perceived threat. I want to catch Adalia Wood more than I want to coddle your feelings. I couldn't have stopped her today, because it took your sexy ass too long to come tell me about her. And I am *not* like Pritchett."

Sexy. Did he mean that? Idiot, that doesn't matter right now.

Rather than cower on the bench, she stood and stepped

forward until her toes bumped his. Angry heat bounced off him, but she refused to give in. "You think today was *my* fault?"

"Maybe you could have acted quicker."

"Maybe you could have told me what was going on so I could have been on the look out. I would've known who she was so I could react faster!"

"You—"

"Couldn't have done anything any differently!" She shoved him back a step. "I stepped into the hallway and saw a silhouetted woman I didn't get a good look at until it was too late. What was I supposed to do, magically transport myself to you while barricading her retreat?"

"Maggie—"

"My sister and daughter were in the next room. She was in the car before I figured out who she was. My priorities were dead on." She bit her tongue to keep herself from voicing the colorful string of four-letter words that would help nothing. But he was wrong.

"Here's the long and short of it, Mags. You agreed to my living here." His voice quieted to normal. His eyes softened. "You wanted to feel safer. I'll make sure you are."

"Your presence didn't stop her from waltzing in the front door."

"No, but it will not happen again." Confidence rode his deep-timbered growl.

Her anger drained as fast as it had built to a boil. Her temper was hot, but generally subsided quickly. "Does she want me dead?"

"If she doesn't get what she wants."

"What does she want?"

"Not sure."

"You know more than you're telling."

"And I'll no doubt piss you off again before I have it all figured out. If I notice something off I probably won't take the time to ask you politely to do something." He held up a hand when she opened her mouth. "But I'll try to give you as much of an explanation as I can."

"Start with what you found in the office?"

"No."

"Why?"

"It only raises more questions. Potentially painful ones."

"Maybe I could help you answer them."

"No."

She stepped around the immovable mass of man in front of her and paced the floor. "You treat this like a top secret mission. I deserve to know."

"I intend to keep my job, which means I'm not telling you." He spun on his heel and headed to the kitchen door. He paused and grinned back at her. "By the way, I love the bag."

Mouth agape, she watched him shut the door. What had just happened?

She wouldn't cost him his job, but a killer had walked in and out of her home as cool as a privileged cucumber. Maggie and her family were at risk every moment Adalia was free. With or without Harte in the house, she was not equipped for emotional warfare with a killer.

Or the sexy detective awakening her desires.

Listening to the pounding rain, which had threatened for the last week, Maggie stretched out beside Jared on his bed. Dressed in one of Mike's shirts with his eyes drooping as sleep dragged him under, Jared curled at her side. The hint of a smile quirked his lips, but still not a full smile. That was something she hadn't seen since Mike's death.

She sighed as she looked at the picture on Jared's wall Mike had painstakingly painted. It was a strange and colorful glow-in-the-dark view of the arctic tip as it should have looked three thousand years ago. He'd even included symbols around the edges, hiding them within the images while claiming they were a legend—like on a man. Breathtaking in its detail, it was the last thing he'd done for Jared. Maggie worried it rooted him in his grief, or maybe she did it by keeping him too close.

Jared snuggled deeper into her, his thin fingers fidgeting a shirt button in sleep. He had no idea danger had crossed their doorstep. She would make sure it stayed that way.

Tomorrow she was taking the kids to stay with her parents, out of harm's way until things settled down. She wasn't sure if it was a good decision or bad—the three of them hadn't been apart for the last year—so she'd taken tonight to assure Jared the visit would be like old times. The assurance had been more for her sake.

A cry from the nursery sounded on the cordless monitor. Her feet hadn't hit the floor before Emma stopped crying. She still wanted to check before going to the office to work out an HTML issue she was having.

She stepped on a Transformer on the way out of Jared's room and muttered about the new hole in her foot. She'd clean the room properly while he was gone. He'd done a pretty good job, but it still needed some help. Books needed to be re-sorted, marker lids needed to be matched properly, and toys were just shoved onto shelves and into the toy box. They needed straightening. She'd find similar disarray in his drawers and closet.

A thud and soft curse from Emma's room snapped her head up. Harte was in his room. Who was in Emma's?

Harte had assured her the kids were safe, but no one had thought Adalia would walk through her front door either. Anxiety dancing along her nape, she pushed the nursery door open.

One step into the room, she jerked to a stop.

The badass detective had removed his shirt and exchanged his jeans for a pair of loose-fitting, drawstring pants that hung low on his hips. His broad back was tan and smooth. She'd had her hands on that back when he'd kissed her. Each chiseled muscle rippled as he swayed with Emma.

"Come on, sweetie." His normally rough and husky voice

sounded smooth as cream as he soothed her fretful infant. "Don't fuss. Mommy will come as soon as she finishes with Jare."

Emma continued to fuss. Harte continued to talk. Maggie continued to stare, and smile at the tenderness he showed her daughter. Her belly quivered at Harte's sexy, softer side. A man that good with kids deserved his own.

"Now, Ems, if you don't stop crying, I'm going to have to take drastic measures." He stopped swaying and looked down at Emma. "I'll have to sing. I don't think you'll like that."

Maggie tried to suck back the sudden laugh. Maybe if he'd said it in something other than a syrupy, singsong voice it would've carried some weight.

Harte spun on his heel. The sudden movement shocked Emma silent. Maggie's hand flew up to cover her mouth. Not in her wildest imaginings had he looked this good shirtless.

His eyes—the bright, clear blue that looked like the sky after a rain—always appeared to know her thoughts before she had them.

She devoured the sight of bulging muscles, picturing her fingers tracing each perfectly sculpted inch of him. A light dusting of sandy brown hair trailed down to the hard abs. She wanted to run her fingers over him and down his thin treasure trail.

She could virtually feel his skin glide under her fingers as she familiarized herself with his body. Her stomach did a round-off-back-handspring combo. She tried to swallow the lump in her throat, but it refused to budge. *Yummalicious.* It was the only way to describe his body.

Taking a deep breath, she gathered her self-control. When she lowered her hand to her side, it shook lightly. His state of dress, or rather undress, and the sight of him holding Emma in the remembered security and strength of those arms aroused her. *Lucky kid.*

Her feelings for Mike had evolved quietly and gradually from a close friendship. Nothing about Harte was gradual or quiet, which probably explained some of the appeal. She'd often fantasized about a life with more spark.

Space. She needed space. Now.

She should take Emma, who had drifted back to sleep, send Harte back to his side of the house, lock herself in her room and hope it was enough to keep her from straying to him. His bed.

She took another deep breath, stepped forward.

"Harte…"

"Mags…"

They spoke at the same time. Whatever she'd been planning to say flew from her mind. His raspy voice was back, and it scraped along her sensitized nerve endings like a soothing caress. She tilted her head and studied him. "Why do you call me Mags?"

Harte shrugged his shoulders. "Just seems to fit."

"I've never tolerated anyone calling me that." A childhood memory had the corner of her mouth twitching. "I nearly broke a boy's nose for it in middle school."

Harte raised his eyebrows and patted Emma on the back. The gesture felt more like a promise to continue calling her Mags than any kind of surprise. "Why do you call me Harte?"

With a small grin, she tossed his words back at him. "Just seems to fit."

Silence invaded, arousal hummed, as they stood watching each other. Her humor leaked out of the situation like air hissing from a tire. Too bad Emma was asleep and couldn't distract them.

She motioned toward Emma and sighed. "Why are you doing this?"

"I heard her crying." He kept swaying as if Emma still needed soothing. "You were busy."

She'd wanted to know why he was inserting himself in her life, making it impossible to not like him or want to lean on him. He may not be doing it on purpose, but neither was he interested in satisfying her hunger for a man's devotion. Even if he was it couldn't happen. His job was just too deadly. "Thanks for the help."

"You seem surprised."

Huh? Oh, right. "Most men, especially single ones, are hesitant when it comes to babies." She'd have guessed him to be one the day he'd first seen Emma. "You handle her like you've done it a thousand times."

"I like kids." He brushed a finger over one of Emma's angelic cheeks. Maggie couldn't see his eyes, but somehow knew that like his voice they had darkened with sadness. "My sister Laurel has a daughter about this size."

Maggie's eyes widened. Laurel had called during one of Harte's runs for more boxes. They'd talked for a while, but Maggie had gotten the impression there was a distance between them. The pride in his voice suggested she rethink her judgment.

She held out her arms for him to give Emma to her. "Thank you for letting me finish with Jared."

"No problem." As he moved away after passing Emma over, his hand brushed Maggie's breast. There was nothing sexual about the touch, and yet an electric jolt shot through her. Looking into his eyes, she knew he felt it too.

Harte cleared his throat and stepped aside, out of her way, but not out of the room. Wishing she didn't want to ask why he hovered, she settled Emma in her crib.

Thunder boomed. The lights went dark.

Maggie jerked. Her heart lurched and slammed into her ribs.

Adalia? She shook off the thought. *No.* The main breaker probably flipped. It was normal during bad storms. She needed to have it replaced. Sighing, she straightened, stepped back, and slammed into Harte. Lightning zapped her.

"I need..." She tried to step to the left, but bumped into his arm.

Moving to the right, she hit his other arm. Since he left her no choice, she braced her hands on the crib and shoved back against his chest hoping to budge him—all six-plus feet of him. Too much longer of touching him and she'd melt into the floor, her brain would turn to Jell-o and she'd begin drooling.

At least then he wouldn't be invading her space and senses.

When he didn't budge, she stepped closer to the crib. The move broke the contact so she could no longer feel his body, yet his heat and scent, something spicy that made her want to lean in, bury her face against him just smell him for hours, still enveloped her.

"Harte, is there a reason you're hovering?" She applauded herself for not sounding as erotically stimulated as she felt.

"Come with me." He grabbed her hand.

By the time he stepped back enough to let her turn, her eyes had adjusted to the dark enough to see his gun. Where had that come from? Because it hadn't been tucked in his pants. Did he have a pocket in his skin? She trailed after him, not that his pulling on her hand gave her a choice. "What's with you and the gun?"

"I always have it." He stopped outside Emma's room. "Close her door."

Maggie rolled her eyes and did as he asked—ordered. "You're being pushy."

"Deal with it." His tone held a smile, telling her he remembered their talk, wasn't changing, was in fact enjoying pushing her buttons.

As soon as Emma's door latched, he pulled Maggie down the hall and checked her room. Images of them on her bed, rolling in the covers, flashed in her head before they were moving back up the hall to Jared's room. In the office, Harte made sure the blinds were still closed and checked every possible hiding place—including beneath the desk.

She tried telling him it was likely just a breaker. He brushed her off.

His proximity minimized the fear his search had closing in on her. The doubt telling her she was wrong about the breaker.

Had Adalia really gotten into the house again? What was she after?

When he started to pull her back into the hall, she jerked her arm free. The bullying demands and nagging whys and what-ifs had to cease.

"What the hell are you doing?" He grabbed her hand again. Frustration tightened his grip, but he didn't hurt her.

"You may enjoy trolling around in the dark with your gun, but I'm getting a flashlight." She pulled free and inched her way to the desk, not knowing where all his boxes were. "Besides, it's easier to see the breaker box with a flashlight."

"How do you know it's a breaker?"

I don't, thanks to you! I'm trying not to be scared. "We almost always lose power in strong storms."

"We, as in you, or we, as in the neighborhood?"

"Me." She pulled her pink Magnum flashlight out of the pen holder, twisted it on, and shined it to the floor. Slowly, she slid the beam of light up his body. He was hard everywhere. Absolutely everywhere. Dark, half-dressed, aroused. Her own body hummed a hungry response.

"The breaker box needs to be replaced," she choked out.

"Fine. We'll check it." He held his hand out. Did he honestly think they were cozy enough to walk through the house holding hands like a love-struck couple?

"Fine." Ignoring his hand, she started to move past him with the light.

He grabbed her wrist, slid his hand down to grip hers and pulled her behind him. "After you humor me and we check the rest of the house."

Arguments tripped over themselves at her tongue's tip, but she didn't want to admit he might be right. And all right, his strong hand around hers was a seductive distraction. Then he pulled her right up to his side.

Too close.

His scent wouldn't let her breathe. She wanted nothing more than to bury her face in any part of him and breathe him deep. No! It wasn't right. He was here to do a job. Sure, he'd pulled her to his body, but that didn't mean he was inviting her to taste every inch of him.

He was aroused, but not necessarily because of her. Still, she wanted to wallow in the warmth and pure maleness oozing from him. Too bad she'd probably burn up faster than a re-entry into Earth's atmosphere.

His spice had her stomach muscles clenching. She was probably playing with fire, tempting him to kiss her again, but she couldn't resist.

She drew in a slow breath. *Ooooh.* He smelled delicious. She'd gone loony, but he was too potent for a woman's peace of mind. What was he thinking running around with pants only held up by a tiny string, no shirt and a gun?

She rolled her eyes. Wicked as her thoughts may be, resisting the urge to test the limits of the tightly leashed power humming beneath his skin wasn't an option. She justified curiosity by telling herself she needed to know the boundaries to avoid getting burned. She needed to know the line not to cross if she hoped to guard her heart.

His grip on her arm held her so close she bumped into his back every time he hesitated. The imprint of his body remained when he moved away. The more times they brushed, the more heightened her senses became to his flesh against her own. The longer her skin took to stop tingling.

He moved toward the kitchen and dining room. Another boom of thunder shook the house. Maggie yelped and clutched his arm.

"Retract the claws." Tension tightened his voice. "It was just thunder."

"Right." Stepping back, she told herself to chill out. Then again, with his suspicious mind amping up her nerves how could she?

He checked the back door before moving toward the garage. "Where's the breaker box?"

"Far wall in the corner." She took a deep breath and stayed

close as he dragged her behind him. When he tripped over Jared's scooter, she lurched forward and slammed into his back almost taking them both to the floor. He never released his grip as he regained his footing and kept her upright.

At the box, necessity had him freeing her so he could open the small door and flip the breakers. Light shone into the garage from the kitchen. So it had been the storm. Relief eased her fear, and made room for the irritation. Irritation caused by Harte's reaction to the brushing touches of their skin—or rather his lack of reaction. Irritation that he'd kissed her passionately, twice, and now acted with complete disinterest.

Not a word. No indication an inferno sizzled through his veins like the one raging in hers. Aside from an earlier shiver, he gave no indications she affected him, and it pissed her off.

She was insane. She didn't want an involvement, but neither could she ignore the way her body screamed for his. The passion when they kissed couldn't have been imagined. Could it? *Only one way to know.*

Biting her tongue, she reached out to run the tip of her nail down the length of his spine. His muscles twitched. Before she reached the waist of his pants, he spun and pinned her beneath his body to the hood of his car. His hands gripped her hips, his fingers digging lightly into her butt, he held her close.

Not unaffected.

The evidence pressed against her hip. She wrapped her hands around his neck and angled her head to meet his eyes in the semi-darkness. His gaze smoldered.

"You're begging for trouble, Mags."

Probably so, but in this moment she wanted his kind of trouble. She arched, rubbed against his erection. "How so?"

Harte invaded her physical space and dominated her mind with his scent. His head swooped down and with unerring aim, his mouth covered hers. Shockwaves of pleasure and heat coursed through her body.

Her panties dampened. With a racing heart and tingling skin burning beneath his touch, she'd never been more ready.

Her ears rang and the garage spun like a carnival ride. She gasped. His tongue swept inside, exploring every inch of her mouth. His tongue tangoed with her tongue. He devoured her. His touch scorched her brain, short-circuited thought and left only instinct.

He ran a hand up her side and palmed her breast. His thumb circled her nipple, hardening it more. She moaned into his mouth, wrapped a leg over his and slid it up to his hip. With her hands buried in his thick hair, she pulled him closer, molded her body to his, wished there were no clothes separating them.

So hot. She wanted to get closer.

He grabbed her thigh and rocked against her—long and hard. He tasted her mouth before he withdrew to bite her lower lip. She traced her tongue over his upper lip, grabbed his hair, pulled him back.

For once in her life she held passion in her grasp. She didn't want to let it go.

Thunder boomed.

Harte jerked his head up.

Pointing his gun toward the overhead door as if he expected Adalia to appear, his body kept her in place. His labored breath vibrated through her and he couldn't blame it on the sudden boom. Maggie pouted at the sudden loss of his thrilling kisses and the invasion of reality.

If they hadn't been jarred from the moment, if he released his control for more than a brief moment here or there, she would dissolve and give him anything he wanted. In return, he'd give her the fire and passion she had long fantasized about, but in the process she feared he would take over her body and heart.

Not possible. She couldn't risk her heart to a man who would soon walk out the door.

Chapter Six

Careful not to touch her and further incite his arousal, BD escorted Maggie to her bedroom and then hustled back to his. At the soft snick of the latch, he leaned against the door and slid to the floor with his legs stretched straight toward the bed. His shoulders dropped. His head fell between his knees.

What had he been thinking?

He should've been focused on the house and everyone's safety. Instead, he let her bait him until her sultry voice had images of her naked and writhing popping into his head, driving away reason. Nothing about their situation made the possibility realistic.

Still, one touch low on his back and she hit his sweet spot. The spot that melted his knees like candle wax beneath a flame. The spot that made his stomach clench in desire. The spot no woman had discovered. His arousal had been instant. His reaction instinctive. Pinning her to the car, though, nearly forgetting everything for the sake of the promised pleasure had been a monumental mistake.

Leaving the Adalia puzzle unsolved would only put Maggie in more danger. Everyone would be better off if he stayed focused on her safety and stopping a repeat of Adalia's previous run.

He had replayed the day of Mike's death countless times since that day. Nothing could have been done differently. Nothing could have saved Mike once Adalia had been tipped off that they were on to her. Mike Sullivan had been her retaliation.

BD pinched the bridge of his nose. Maybe the crash hadn't been an accident. Depending on the connection to Sullivan, Adalia may have wanted to silence him. The same could be said for Maggie.

They needed to set a trap for Adalia, but to do that they

needed to know what she sought. Maggie was the key. BD would find the answer, Maggie would never know the details, and he would keep his promises to a dying man. Then he'd get away from the woman who made him want to put the man in him before the cop.

Moving to his desk, BD booted up his laptop. A Google search for the few key words they had wouldn't narrow the field much. And they needed the prison records to figure out who was helping Adalia. The warden's email had only had a recap of the records, which wasn't enough.

BD typed in search words dealing with keys and power. Curiosity had him adding linguist to the search list.

Results one through ten of five thousand, two hundred and fifty. "This'll be fun."

He changed the search parameter to include *magic key* and hit enter.

Results one through ten of three thousand and seventy.

"Two thousand less, assuming I'm on the right path," he muttered. "Time wasted if I'm wrong."

He skimmed the screen while his mind drifted back to Maggie.

For her, everyone else's needs came first. She'd shown her steel-coated spine by standing silently while he pounded the punching bag and how she'd protected her sister and kids from the encroaching ugliness. Physical and emotional strength got her through pregnancy and single parenthood without a day of support from her husband.

You could have stopped it. You should have stopped it.

Her earlier words swam back. If he'd stopped Adalia, she wouldn't have been widowed. That truth was on him. Yeah, he'd missed something the first time around. He wouldn't make the same mistake again.

Thinking about how things might have been was as effective as a shower curtain on a cellar in a tornado. Only focus and hard work would solve the case, and again the answers may rest, possibly to his demise, with Maggie

Sullivan. He opened a new document, began listing what he knew, what he'd observed about her.

Obsessive compulsive. She cleaned things someone else had just done, the food in the pantry was sorted by type and then size, and she stocked condoms in the guest bedroom, now his room. She had an eye for details, though at times too much.

She met chaos with a cool head. Mostly. How far could she be pushed?

Adalia's note had said the cops had gotten in the middle. Meaning him and Craig and the day they'd caught her. It seemed a logical leap that if Mike was the professor Adalia referred to he'd been working on something before his death. As a linguist, it could have been a translation. But what sort of translation was worth killing over?

There had to be answers in the house. Where could a man hide something from Maggie?

Hoping she would stay in her room, BD shut down his computer and went to walk the house. Sitting still for too long unnerved him, so he did what he'd seen Maggie do each night he'd watched her house. He double-checked every door and window lock and made sure the blinds were closed.

On a pass through the living room he rearranged the pillows on the couch. Grinning, he shifted the magazines on the coffee table from the left corner to the right and fanned them out. He wanted to see how long it took her to put things back to her way. *How OCD is she?*

Taking up post at the front window, watching the street through barely slatted blinds, he tried to think of an angle he was missing. Focus evaded him.

Her soft fragrance of vanilla and roses floated up and tickled his nose. His blood surged faster. His body remembered the feel of her beneath him. He'd been so close to losing himself in her. So close to taking everything she offered.

Refusing to think about why her scent lingered in his mind, BD stared out at the darkened street. Adalia knew he was there, waiting, which would make setting a trap more challenging. It was worth it though to keep a closer eye on things. On Maggie.

The vanilla scent grew stronger. He gripped the bridge of his nose, but too late to avoid the aromatic induced awakening. The drawback to being inside rested in his attraction to her—in her ability to distract him by simply existing.

Kissing her in the garage had been bad. Pinning her underneath him... His system fired up again at the memory of her soft curves pressing into him, her leg hooked on his hip, her hands clutching at him. He wouldn't repeat the lapse, but neither would he forget the pleasure he'd felt with her in his arms.

"Anything exciting happening?" The huskily whispered words had his heart double timing.

"F—!" He spun around to face Maggie. No wonder he'd smelled her. "Where'd you come from?"

"My bed." She leaned against the wall on the other side of the window. Her hair hung loose over her shoulders in thick waves that almost reached her waist.

"What are you doing out here?" He fisted his hands to keep from reaching for her. To keep from discovering how her hair felt in his hands. Didn't she know how distracting she was? Or was that why she'd come back out?

"I don't sleep much. I heard you moving around."

"A warning would've been nice." He tapped his fingers against his leg to keep from reaching out for her. Somewhere in the world was a man who would one day be able to kiss her whenever he wanted. He'd know nothing bad would happen if he got lost in her. BD wasn't that man.

"I could say the same."

"Sorry?"

"Earlier. I knew you would be keeping an eye on things, but it would've been nice to know you intended to prowl the house every night with a loaded weapon."

Her hushed voice in the darkened house filled his mind with images of her wrapped around him. He gave himself a mental slap. "Useless if it isn't loaded."

"Are you going to slink around in the middle of the night every night until she's caught?"

"If that's what it takes."

And no matter how much he admired Maggie, from the tip of her head to the bottom of her killer legs capable of landing lethal spinning kicks, BD wouldn't admit to anything else. Why he was really here, or how he wanted everything and everyone to disappear so he could have her to himself, would remain his secrets.

"I'm good at puzzles. I might be able to help you figure out what she wants."

"No." His suspicions couldn't touch her.

"Fine. Go back to watching the empty street." Dismissal or maybe disappointment dripped from her tone but she didn't turn away.

"Mags, I promised to keep you safe." He brushed her hair off her shoulder. Sparks of arousal shot through him. "I'm trying to keep it."

"You can't protect me from the mental torments Adalia keeps springing on me. The iPod was one of the worst."

"I can imagine and I'm sorry about that." He cocked his head to the side. A new thought occurring to him. "You saw Adalia's silhouette?"

"Yes."

"And the person driving Mike's car that day?"

"Was a man." Maggie's chin jutted out slightly. Her back stiffened. "She has a partner?"

"Seems so." *Whoever was helping her didn't stop at getting her out of prison.* He'd also gotten his hands on a car that was supposed to be destroyed and fixed it up enough to torment her.

Adalia had known Mike's car would screw with Maggie, but not as much as a personal gift or the knowledge there were two people possibly after her. He could think of no way to ease her mind. "Listen, why don't you try to get some sleep?"

"Can't. Every sound makes me jump. If I close my eyes now…" She walked to the couch and sat, clutching a pillow to her stomach. She'd already fixed the pillows and magazines. "Sleep isn't going to happen for me."

BD knelt in front of her and captured her gaze. "Do you trust me to watch the house? To keep you and the kids safe?"

"Yes."

No hesitation, just a blind faith he wasn't sure he deserved. He'd be damned if he let her down. "Then try to get some sleep."

Reaching for the other throw pillows on the couch, he piled them up. "Lie here. Read if it'll help, but try not to dwell on what you can't control."

Her eyebrows scrunched together with worry and fear. "Whatever Adalia's after, I'm catching the brunt of her torments. Am I supposed to ignore that? To feel nothing?"

He felt the impact of Adalia's manipulations through Maggie. The urge to tell her everything in hopes of erasing her fear surged up. Her knowing wouldn't make things easier on her. Stopping Adalia would.

"If you could, I wouldn't like you so much. It would mean you're hard." He picked Maggie's feet up off the floor and raised them to the sofa, half-forcing her to lie down. "She isn't going to hurt you."

When she settled into the cushions, he pulled the blanket from the back of the sofa over her and prepared himself for a sleepless night. If it meant he went without sleep for days or weeks, Adalia would see the backside of bars again.

Hell would become a new polar cap before he let anything else happen to Maggie and her kids.

Maggie half expected it when she'd told him she was taking the kids to her parents. It was logical, but Harte's actions—his approach—crossed a line. She pulled into the garage and parked beside his shiny black Audi sedan. The unfamiliar, violent desire to bust something on it surprised her. Taking a deep breath, she reminded herself to stay calm and in control.

She'd been looking forward to a few hours away from drama, stress and dark thoughts. Harte robbed her of that. With his name sounding like a curse in her head, she got out of the Tahoe and headed into the house. *Calm. Control.*

"Yep. Thanks." He slid his cell phone into his pocket and closed the refrigerator door as she stepped inside. He waved with a bottle of water in his hand. "How was the farm?"

As if he didn't know. She went to the refrigerator and pulled out a water bottle. "I want an explanation."

"What?"

She slowly closed the door and turned back to face him. Sharing a house made avoiding certain intimacies and daily rituals impossible. Common courtesy still mattered. "Living with you, your caveman attitude and secrets is one thing. You feeling entitled to set one of your lackeys on me for surveillance is another."

"I'm not... What are you talking about?"

Ignorance did *not* suit him. He couldn't pull it off. Swallowing a drink, she let the cool water lower her temperature. Loosening her grip on her emotional control would only lead to the disintegration of her physical control, which was not a viable option. She just might give in to the earlier urge to bust up his car.

"I'm talking about me being followed to my family's farm?"

"What?" His eyes widened. "Someone followed you?"

No way did she buy his shock was genuine. "A gorgeous man, looking remarkably like Officer McClain, in a mostly restored fifty-seven Oldsmobile Cutlass tailed me all day. I thought about pulling over and asking him out if he pulled up behind me. He is, after all, erotic romance novel hot."

"You wouldn't have." He spat the retort as if it were an angry dare.

She shrugged.

"If you ever pull a stunt like that I will cuff you to the nearest bed."

"Then McClain would know where to find me."

His cobalt eyes frosted. His face set into a granite hard stare. "Neither of you would find the experience as pleasurable as something you might read in those novels of yours."

Hmm. He was jealous. And not as closed off as she'd thought. "So, you don't deny you had me followed."

He took a drink and met her gaze. "What makes you think he was following you?"

Maggie raised her pinkie finger. "I've met McClain. I noticed the car at the edge of the housing division and remember thinking with a little more money, maybe a new paint job and some shinier rims, it would be a sweet ride and worth considerable money."

She watched Harte steadily as she raised her ring finger. "Your man's good. Most people would have a hard time spotting him. I grew up with men who loved old cars, and one of them spent considerable time in the military. I've been taught how to notice things."

Harte licked his lips and grinned as if she amused him. His sharp gaze never left hers. "What else did you notice?"

She added her middle finger to indicate her next point. "I took an exit a little past the normal one."

She'd stayed in the left lane, waiting until the last possible second to weave through the scattered cars to take the exit. The Cutlass had tried to follow her, but other drivers had blocked his path.

"So, what did you discover when you came up on him from behind?"

Harte might have pulled the ruse off if he hadn't tensed up. He was quite easy to read when she paid attention. Maggie lifted her index finger and wiggled the four. "I didn't come up behind him. I took a different route to the farm. Imagine my surprise when I found him waiting at the end of the property line as I left to come home."

The feigned humor faded from Harte's face. He couldn't deny what he'd done.

She leaned against the counter. "Explain to me how Officer McClain knew where I was headed if you didn't assign him to watch me."

She didn't give him time to answer. "The way I see it... You think I'm involved in something but won't say what, so you're treating me like a suspect."

She quirked her brow and dared him to lie. She wasn't backing down. Her days of bending to everyone else's wishes were over. She had regained her balance and rediscovered her spine.

"Fine. I had him follow you. I don't think of you as a suspect, but I made you a promise. I don't take my promises lightly." Eerily enough it was something he and Adalia had in common. Only her promises were criminal.

"You could have told me. You didn't have to invade my privacy."

"Couldn't be helped."

"Bull. You had more than one choice when you knew where I was going. If you felt the need to keep that close an eye on me you could have asked to join us."

"Didn't want to intrude."

With her ire passing, Maggie noticed a picture frame in the corner of a cabinet had been moved. Her left eye twitched as she went to straighten it. "You mean you wanted me watched while you searched my house. You betrayed the trust you asked for."

"It's not like that, Mags."

He stood in front of her and lied to her face. For the first time, the sound of her name on his lips sickened her. "You're here so it's easier to blend in with the neighbors and to be closer should something happen. You've not been given open access to my life."

"That's not what this is."

"Really?" She crossed her ankles and arms. "Then explain it."

"I can't." He set his bottled water on the counter. "But I was justified."

"Wrong, Detective. *What* you did is one thing. *How* you went about it is another." She pursed her lips and breathed deep.

"No." Cold determination laced his voice. "Some things are justified."

She didn't care that his jaw twitched with leashed anger. She wanted to pummel him.

"I get it." She shrugged. "I had a lot of time to think on the way home."

"What do you get, Mags?"

"Adalia wants something I have. You won't tell me what, though my help figuring it out could help you catch her faster. So rather than trust me you're treating me like a villain while hoping to get lucky before I figure too much out."

"I can't help what you believe."

Another lie. "You could with a little honesty." She worked at leveling her heart rate to stay in control. The pounding wouldn't slow.

"I need you to trust me to keep you safe until Adalia's back behind bars." Sincerity glimmered in his eyes, softening her resolve to fight him.

Still, she wasn't the weak, helpless woman relying on the strong man to guide her. He could stand between her and a killer sure. Order her around, no. "If I know who you're after, why can't you tell me the rest?"

"It goes back to my promises."

"You haven't promised me anything that would stop you."

"Not all of my promises were made to you."

Who then? Who could have asked him other than her? He wouldn't tell her. Fine. She would find out on her own. "If you didn't have me followed because you suspect me of something then why?"

Harte winced a little, but didn't look away. "Safety."
"So I'm Adalia's target."
Any hope of sleep vanished with the scary truth.

Chapter Seven

Satisfied he wouldn't drip blood everywhere, something that would no doubt send Maggie into a whirl of OCD cleaning, BD wrapped a green towel around his waist, stuck his head out the hallway door of his bathroom and listened for signs of her location. He'd seen a first-aid kit in the kitchen and with luck could grab it and get back to his room before seeing her.

Silence greeted him. A good sign, but Maggie would be around somewhere. She always was. Easing down the hall in a near tiptoe walk, he went to the kitchen. One step into the room he froze.

Maggie. Bent over, pulling a pot out of the cabinet, pale peach slacks stretched across her hips, enhancing her curves.

Damn.

He hardened. The towel tented. He rolled his eyes and stifled a moan. If she turned, she'd see what the towel couldn't hide, so keeping a wary eye out, he sidestepped toward the sink.

She straightened and turned. Her eyes darted over him and her jaw hardened. With no more than a few feet separating them, he saw every miniscule change on her face—flushing cheeks, twitching lips, darkening irises.

His hand throbbed with renewed force of his pumping blood.

Suddenly, as if a stick of dynamite exploded behind her, Maggie slammed the skillet on the counter, jumped across the room and grabbed his towel-wrapped hand. She pushed him toward the table and into a chair. "What did you do?"

A pulse of something—an odd mix of searing pain and enjoyment—sliced through his palm. He preferred her reaction to be to his naked body, but would take what he could get as long as she kept touching him.

"Dropped the razor. The blade broke in half." He used his free hand to secure the towel at his waist.

She licked her enticing lips. Her fingers brushed his arm as she raised his hand.

His brain flipped a breaker in its intelligence box. If much more blood flowed out of his brain, he'd pass out at her feet. "I cut myself."

"I gathered." She pulled a chair close to his and began unwinding the bloody towel from his hand. "Was all this really necessary?"

Is it necessary for you to touch me and feel nothing? He watched her fuss over him and wondered if he'd moved to heaven or hell. This case was not going to end well. He wanted her, painfully, but as long as she wasn't interested, he had no choice but to stay away from her. Who was he kidding? He had no choice anyway.

It would be fun trying to convince her though. *I really have lost too much blood.*

Scanning her face, the way she licked her bottom lip before sucking it between her teeth, he grew harder. He got a sexual reaction out of her when he pinned her to the couch or the car, but the sight of him wet...wrapped in only a towel and obviously aroused, did nothing to her.

Great. A man always wanted to be slapped in the face with his lack of appeal to a sexy woman. As much as it grated on his nerves that she seemed to have turned off her desire, that she could turn it off, he reminded himself again it was a good thing. She couldn't mean too much to him, or he wouldn't be able to protect her.

Personal involvements only complicated things.

More than her looks, which rocked harder than Godsmack, attracted him. Her mannerisms and the way she handled herself were others. He'd made a promise to her husband, and it had nothing to do with stretching her across the table and spreading himself over her like cream cheese on a bagel.

He cleared his throat. "At the time it was."

"Why didn't you just put some antiseptic and a bandage on it?" She shook her head as she went to the sink, wet a washcloth, and retrieved the first-aid kit from the cabinet.

"There weren't any in the drawers." Her moves were logical and efficient. Cool control coated sizzling sensuality.

"You could've asked where they were." She picked his hand up again and wiped away the blood.

"I wasn't dressed." Not that a towel counted as being dressed, but he hadn't thought she was around.

"I've seen you without a shirt, Harte." She poured antiseptic on the wound. Before he finished his wince, she blew on his palm.

Arousal flooded him as effectively as if she'd spread herself over him. When he swayed in his chair, he grabbed the corner of the table with his free hand. The veins in his head pounded.

"No, Mags." She had to know what he meant. He cleared his throat again and looked over her head, trying to ignore the effect of her touch on his starved soul. The throbbing of his cut paled in comparison to his other aches as every brush of her fingers over his palm made him burn hotter. "I mean I wasn't dressed."

"And you still aren't. I seem to be surviving."

Her cool words washed over him. Though the fire still raged in his veins, he was thinking more clearly. And damn if they weren't fun thoughts. The kids were no longer around to serve as buffers. The distraction could be fun. She couldn't be as unaffected as she now appeared. He'd felt her previous reactions to him.

Unless taking her by surprise was the key to her arousal.

She'd spoken once about Mike's gentleness in all things. He could have been the same way in the bedroom. How sad to live with sex-only-on-Saturday-mornings-and-anything-beyond-missionary-is-hedonistic type thinking. The kitchen was as good a place as any to snap those restraining thoughts.

Perhaps she'd had enough predictability and the thrill of

something different got her off. Whatever made her tick, Maggie Sullivan was not as cool as she pretended and, smart or not, BD would make her react again.

She glued the cut closed, laid a piece of gauze bandage on his palm, and then reached for the first-aid tape. "Had you yelled, I would've told you there's a first-aid kit under the sink."

"I didn't see one."

"Obviously." She pressed the first piece of tape in place and ran her finger over it to make sure it stuck.

He rolled his eyes and leaned in a little closer as her touch echoed within his hungry soul. His breath sent a tendril of her hair waving. The pulse in her throat jumped.

Not unaffected. He smiled as he watched her place the second strip of tape. He leaned closer still as she placed her finger on the end of the tape, ready to press it down like she had the first.

"I like the way you do that." He whispered near her ear and grinned when her pulse rabbited.

She placed the third tape strip in place. Her finger slid over it. He moved even closer. Only a few inches separated them now. "You smell…delicious."

She didn't turn to him, but she swallowed with a barely audible gulp. Oh yeah, he affected her.

She laid the last tape strip on his palm. As she ran her finger over it, he closed another inch. "Such a soft…touch."

Instead of looking away or leaning back, Maggie turned her head. She was close enough that her nose brushed his. Her gaze stared into his. She opened her mouth slightly and blew a warm breath across his lips. "Is that all you…need?"

His stomach jumped. He hadn't thought he could be more aroused, but her single breath and the implication of her words invaded every corner of his hungry body. "Not quite."

"I'm sorry to disappoint you, Harte." She squeezed his injured hand hard enough to start a painful throbbing and moved away to clean up the mess. "You aren't my type."

He sat back in his chair, blinking. The throbbing called back some of the blood that had rushed to his groin. She had been right there, as aroused as him, but she'd easily brushed off the heat.

How?

On her way to the sink she missed a step. When she got there, she fisted her hands on the edge. BD grinned. He may not be the type she wanted to want, but she wanted him.

Slowly and quietly, testing them both, he walked toward her. The smart move would be to return to his room, shave, get dressed and go to work. Drop the idea of shaking her shields with a seduction. He couldn't stop Adalia if he played games all day with Maggie, but the games promised more fun. Wanting a moment of fun, allowing the man to take priority over the cop, wasn't always bad.

He stopped behind her and moved in close enough to look over her shoulder, but stayed far enough away to avoid their bodies brushing. Barely. "Thank you for the nursing, Mags," he whispered. "Next time I want the outfit too."

"Are you trying to crowd me, Harte?" She didn't react. She even sounded composed as she rinsed his blood out of the rag and the towel he'd used.

"Not at all. Just expressing my—" he stepped up, brushing his erection against her, "—gratitude."

Her laugh was an unexpected flow of joy he wanted to hear more often. The shake of her body against his was an awakening. "That's not gratitude."

"Nurses know best." He pressed against her one last time before backing away.

Wanting to see her reaction, he walked backward to the doorway and watched as her breaths came sharply and her hands no longer worked the rag. She stared straight ahead.

He was going to Hell, no two ways about it. May as well make the journey more exciting. "Mags."

"Yes?" Her sweet voice cracked a little.

Grinning, he rested his hands on his waist and waited for

her to turn and face him, which she finally did. "Since the sight of my body doesn't affect you one way or the other, I'll not bother next time."

He flicked a hand and sent the towel cascading to the floor. Cocking a brow, he gave her a completely unobstructed view.

She gasped. Her eyes widened. Arousal stamped her flushed cheeks. Never again would she be able to claim he left her unaffected.

Whistling, he walked back to his room. Oh yeah, he was going to Hell.

"Son of a…" BD fisted his hands against the urge to throw his computer, or anything else close at hand, across the crowded bullpen. "It has to be a dirty cop."

"Could be a prison guard." Craig—reading the prison records they'd finally received—flipped a pen between his fingers.

"Both." Having confirmation from Captain Winchester that Adalia had to have had inside help with her escape, BD ping-ponged between rage and the futility of having no real answers. He looked again at the prison logs. "No cops were signed in at the time."

"A guard could've let one pass."

"Or it could have been set up from before." Winchester was going to have the guards on duty at the time of Adalia's escape interviewed, but BD wasn't convinced they would find anything. Typically speaking, the ones who got caught up in bribes were good at lying and covering their tracks.

"Detectives."

BD raised a brow at Officer Mac McClain as he approached in jeans and a dark blue T-shirt. "McClain."

"I'm off shift. Thought I'd see if you needed any help." Mac stood ramrod straight, with his legs braced slightly apart and his hands behind his back, in a military at-ease stance. A sheepish blush stained his cheeks.

BD tapped his pen against the papers in front of him.

"Sir, I'm sorry about that." Mac lifted his chin slightly. "I've placed an extra change of civvies in my car should I be needed again on short notice."

Craig coughed out a laugh. "Mac, relax."

"Sir, I screwed up." He remained at attention.

"It wasn't your fault," BD offered. Maggie had known about Adalia and, though he hadn't admitted it to her, he could have told her about a tail. Or at least expected her to be on the lookout. "She sees too much."

"Yes, sir."

BD dropped his pen and squeezed the bridge of his nose. "Sit down."

McClain nodded once and followed the order keeping his back ramrod straight.

"Mac, you've been out of the military a few years now. Your record from the Austin PD is stellar, and you've done a great job since coming on here."

"Thank you, sir."

"I'm guessing you joined the military as soon as you graduated high-school to get away from something."

He hesitated momentarily before answering. "Yes, sir."

"Don't take this the wrong way, but if you don't loosen up and stop addressing us as if we're your commanding officers, I'm going to kick your ass."

"Sorry, sir?"

"Like that. Call me BD or Harte." He pointed at Craig, who grinned as he kicked back in his chair still flipping his pen. "He's Craig or Harrison."

"Yes, si—BD. I'll work on it." Mac stood and started to walk away, but turned back with a grin. "For the record, I don't think you could kick my ass."

Craig burst out laughing.

BD smiled slowly. "See, that's more like it. And anytime you want to test your theory, you let me know. I'd love the workout"

"Will do. And I'll do a drive-through of Mrs. Sullivan's neighborhood before I go home."

"Thanks." BD watched McClain walk away and laughed. "He's not going to be on the streets long before he tests for his detective's badge."

"He'll make a good one."

"Yeah." BD picked up the file of notes he'd made copies of. Normally the noise of the bullpen didn't bother him, but today, he needed quiet and space to spread out and think. "I'm going to a conference room. You coming?"

"You know me and puzzles." Craig grabbed his laptop bag, a pen and notepad from his desk.

"Harte!" Pritchett bellowed from across the bullpen. "You find that killer and her papers with your superior know-it-all skills? Or are you too busy banging the pretty brunette?"

BD took a step toward Pritchett before catching sight of a young boy about Jared's age sitting with his mother, a pretty brunette, with another detective. Bruises covered their faces. They shrank back when they looked at him. Whether the mom's fear was from the thought of a killer or BD pounding on someone he'd never know.

Everyone watched, waited, for his reaction. Swallowing his rage, he turned back to his desk and grabbed a rubbery stress ball from a drawer—he had several. He went and knelt before the little boy. Holding the ball out, BD offered an encouraging smile. "When you're scared or angry, use it."

"Playing with balls. Figured you for a cock lover." Pritchett spouted more obscenities.

BD ignored him for the sake of the boy. "Squeeze 'til your hand shakes and your arm hurts. The bad stuff will fade."

The mom rested her hand on her son's shoulder and nodded. He took the ball with a quiet thanks and trembling hands.

Without a second look at Pritchett, BD headed toward the conference room. The day would come for Pritchett to eat his own balls and BD would do the feeding.

"Speaking of Maggie," Craig said as he stepped into the hall with him, "any word on how she's getting along with Officer Phillips today?"

"No." Unwilling to leave her alone, BD had begged an off-duty female detective posing as a visiting friend to stay with Maggie. He had no doubt she would one day call in a return favor. "Phillips will call if there are problems."

Two hours later, having had no success at deciphering Adalia's notes or finding anything else of use, he stepped through the front door and landed smack in the middle of the chaos that seemed to be Maggie's home.

"This has to stop!" Maggie's angry shriek echoed through the tiled hall.

The living room was messy, with knick-knacks moved around or knocked over, couch cushions tossed to the floor, a chair turned over and DVD cases strewn about.

So much for an hour with the punching bag to work off building frustrations.

"Mrs. Sullivan. Maggie." Tension rose Detective Phillips's voice a couple octaves above normal. "We need to call Harte."

Following their voices he rushed toward Maggie's room. She stood just inside the doorway, shaking with rage. Chunks of her habitually perfect braid had been pulled loose—hopefully from her own hands in frustration.

While the living room was messy, her room had been destroyed. Dresser drawers hung half open. Clothes and shredded lingerie were scattered. Her bedding, including the mattress and pillows, had been gutted, and the headboard sported a giant X in what looked to be blood rather than paint. The blinds had been ripped from the windows, leaving a clear view into the empty neighboring house.

This was pure sadistic rage left in Adalia's wake. A calculated evil that would spill over to the public if she wasn't stopped. Fast. Her single-minded focus was the only thing working in their favor. She would miss a step.

"Maggie." He took her hand to pull her into the hallway.

She spun and swung at him with her free hand fisted and eyes wide. He jerked her around, pinned her back to his chest with her arms beneath his before walking her into the hall.

Adrenaline fueled by fear swept through him. Emotional fear.

Maggie was not like other jobs.

"Lora?" He asked the officer for an update.

"We took a walk. Were gone maybe thirty minutes. Got back less than five minutes ago. Maggie found this. We locked up before leaving."

"Have you checked the house?"

"Not yet."

Harte loosened his grip on Maggie enough to turn her to face him, but not enough to let her free. His heart drummed in his ears. He'd had a shitty day with little progress on any of his cases, especially Maggie's, and it had just gotten worse. BD pulled his gun and grabbed Maggie's hand again.

"Seriously, we're doing this again?"

"Yes, and you're staying with me." Adrenaline roared. Possibilities snapped like starved crocodiles. They may have missed Adalia or scared her away. They may also have driven her into hiding. "Lora, check the far side of the house. Closets too."

"On it." The officer pulled her gun from her waist at her back and headed to the office.

"You know, Harte—" Maggie trailed behind him semi-obediently, "—you take this paranoid cop thing too far at times."

"Mags." Her tone didn't relay the casualness her words did and with his patience already close to exhausted for the day, he didn't feel like placating her. Adalia had probably already gone, but it was a chance he couldn't take. "I have a job to do and it includes keeping your stubborn ass alive."

"You think Adalia's still here?"

"I've seen stranger things happen."

Maggie nodded and became agreeable. "Got it."

After a thorough search turned up an empty house, they met back in the living room. "Lora, call Craig, McClain and Lewis. And I want CSIs."

"On it," she said just as she had before and walked away, pulling out her cell phone.

"All right, Mags, here's how this is going to work." He led her to the built-in bookshelves stuffed with romance novels and pointed. "Pick out a book. I'm going to process your house with my team, and I need you to stay out of the way while I'm doing it."

"So you're telling me to pick out a book as if I'm going to be able to relax like nothing's going on?" Her agreeable attitude was slipping away beneath her bristling need to be independent.

"I'm asking you to please pick out a book and go to my room to wait for me. Read. Pretend to read." He shrugged. "I don't give a dam as long as you let me do my job."

She studied his face intently. Her fingers flexed in his. "Answer one question for me first. No qualifications or evasions allowed."

This didn't bode well. She wouldn't ask an easy question he could talk his way out of or around. "One question."

"It's been relatively calm around here the last couple of days in regards to murdered women, animal carcasses and haunting memories from my life with Mike. I was just beginning to relax and now this. How is it Adalia is able to hit me from every angle at the perfect moments?"

It was a tough question, but easier than if she'd asked about the connection to Mike. Still, he had to be careful with his phrasing. To speed things along, he reached up to grab a book from the shelf. Stuck in a corner of a shelf was a small, almost unnoticeable bug. His jaw stiffened until it throbbed.

The destroyed bedroom had netted Adalia nothing so she'd messed up part of the house and planted bugs to see what else she could learn. She wouldn't stop with the privacy invasion until she had what she wanted.

"Because she's gotten lucky. Now, take this book and come with me."

Maggie opened her mouth, no doubt to argue his answer wasn't good enough or that he was being bossy again. He put a finger on her lips to stop her and then led her to his bathroom.

"I want you to take a nice long bath." He motioned for her to stay quiet a little longer. "I realize this tub isn't as luxurious as yours, but it's still quite nice. You said it yourself, you've had a rough few days."

He sat the book on the counter, closed the doors that led to his room and to the hall, turned on the bath water and then searched the room for a bug. "You deserve to relax and let someone else do the worrying for a little bit."

She crossed her arms and leaned against the wall. "Sounds like I should schedule a spa day. Mani, pedi, facial, full-body massage."

He looked up from his search and found her watching him with arched brows and pursed lips. She'd figured out what he was doing and was biding her time. She noticed too much at times, but times like now her awareness worked in his favor.

"I hear you women love those. My mom and sister do."

Once he was satisfied the bathroom was free of bugs, he left the water running and kept his voice low in case he'd missed one. "Adalia is good, but not good enough to do all of this without help. We think she's got someone on the inside, and by that I mean someone on the force. As for how she knows when to strike, I think she's been watching you from very close by—like from the empty rental house next door."

She didn't react physically, which made it impossible to know what she'd do or say next. "And when she's been in the house she's planted bugs."

"Unless you see a need to spy on yourself, yes. So I am asking you to please stay in here or my room while my team processes your house. No phone calls."

"Fine." The mutinous glare in her eyes broadcast her

difficulty with agreeing. "I want an update as soon as you finish."

"I agreed to answer one question. We'll see about more later." She didn't like it, but she'd backed herself into the corner of having to take what he'd give her. Once he had her assurance she would cooperate, he left to join his team.

In the living room, after he pointed out the bug and signaled for a sweep to be done, he lined out what he wanted done with silent instructions for the one in the bookshelf to be left for the time being. He could use it to their favor.

"Maggie's obsessive," BD told them, "so it will be easy to spot anything out of place."

McClain and Lewis were on bug duty. The CSIs would take prints and pictures. He and Craig would take Maggie's room. Lora called in her partner and they would take the house next door.

With everyone heading their own way, he and Craig headed to Maggie's room. Craig pulled his digital camera out and took pictures. Then they settled into the work of sorting through everything to see what Adalia had hidden for Maggie to find.

"This is about more than some papers. It's like Adalia has a personal vendetta to settle."

"She hasn't found what she wants and she isn't seeing the results of getting into Maggie's head." As if the mental rape of destroying her room wasn't a clear enough message, BD picked up a piece of paper pinned to a black lace thong. He didn't need the image in his head of Maggie in a thong. Or the knowledge they seemed to be her preference judging from the scattered clothes. He wouldn't look at her in her proper slacks the same way again.

"Interesting place to leave a note." The humor in Craig's voice snapped him back.

"Very." He unpinned the slip of paper and dropped the panties back onto the pile on the floor. The note shoved the image of Maggie's ass framed in black lace backwards.

*"Mike paid for turning me in. Don't try to outsmart me.
Get me the papers or die."*

—*Adalia*

"Mike turned her in?" Craig paused with a wrinkled T-shirt that might have belonged to a non-OCD Maggie in hand.

"You think he called in the tip about that meeting?"

"It could follow. Maybe he'd decided he was in over his head. Helping stop her was the only way to get out."

Shit. He hadn't wanted to be right about Mike being involved, and if Maggie found out... It would rip her down to the level Adalia wanted her. "We need a more thorough background on Sullivan. I need to finish searching the house, and Maggie is in the way of my doing that."

"You could clue her in and see what she knows."

"No." Involving her could only be a last resort. "At least not yet."

Chapter Eight

"Mags." Exhaustion darkened Harte's eyes when he returned for her.

Checking the clock, Maggie saw she'd been waiting in his room for five hours. More shocking was she'd actually read over half of her newest romantic comedy and the humor had eased some of her tension. "You done?"

"Yeah."

Prepared to spend the night cleaning, she marked her place in the book and headed toward the living room. His team had pawed through her entire house, so she would likely have days of work to do.

She rounded the wall into the living room and stumbled. It was clean. Not just tidy, but clean. Clean to her standards. "Did you guys fingerprint stuff?"

"Yes." He pointed to the bug. "The bedroom's still a little messy, but the rest of the house is clean."

"I'll deal with it." She nodded her understanding and went to see his definition of clean for the rest of the house. Harte didn't follow, as if he knew she needed to face this alone. Every room was as spotless as the living room had been, but she'd saved her room for last.

After a bracing breath, uncertain she wanted to see her room again, she stepped inside and stared.

He'd folded her clothes and stacked them in tidy piles on the dresser. The shredded mattress, bedding and damaged headboard were gone. In their place sat a new mattress on a plain frame. Her knick-knacks had been straightened and all other reminders of the scene were gone. "He…"

Breathing raggedly as her heart shook and her throat grew tight she swiped at her eyes. Unable to mute the hum growing louder and louder in her brain, she shook her head and stared. "He cleaned…"

He had thought of her. Whether he'd known having to clean the mess would shred her guts and rob her of more control or not, he'd dealt with the destruction for her. He'd given her a brief respite from having to handle everything on her own. He'd sheltered her. Yes, there was work still to be done, but she could easily live with letting it wait a little bit.

She bit her bottom lip and walked to the middle of her room. Her hands trembled violently as she reached for an undamaged pillow from the chair. Sinking to the floor, she buried her face in it and curled into a ball. No man had ever touched her like Harte managed to do by cleaning. Tears stabbed her eyes like hot ice picks. Massive sobs racked her body until she ached everywhere.

She cried for the loss of Mike. She cried for Jared's pain. She cried for Emma, who would never know her father. She cried for the rediscovery of herself.

Her neighborhood was no longer the quiet and safe place she'd once thought. Her home had now been invaded and bugged by a killer. Whatever Adalia wanted, Maggie could do nothing to make it all go away.

And as scary as it all was, she had a man in her life, if only temporarily, who had considered her feelings and gone above and beyond in his job. And he'd talked his team into helping. Generally stubborn and demanding, his flashes of thoughtfulness and tenderness struck a chord deep inside and he calmed her as if he'd been doing it for years. He brought to light the reality of what she'd hold out for if she were to ever marry again.

She swiped away a tear and trembled.

It had been less than a week and Harte knew her better than Mike, which was sad considering she'd grown up with her husband.

"Mags." Harte squatted beside her and brushed the hair away from her face.

Looking at him through tear-blurred eyes, she yearned for the freedom to curl into him. To know he'd protect her and his comfort was the kind she could grow to need. Even depend on.

A shiver pranced along her spine. Knowing that kind of connection with Harte, a man who could die any day on his job, wasn't a chance she could take. Opening up again just to lose again... No way.

He settled on the floor, pulled her into his lap and handed her some tissue. He'd apparently taken a quick shower while she wandered the house because he was slightly damp and dressed like he'd been the night the power went out.

Engulfed by helplessness to listen to logic and reason, unable to resist his comfort, she bowed to desire and curled into his warmth. The dusting of hair covering his chest rubbed softly against her cheek. He fit against her perfectly. She hadn't noticed the fit when he'd comforted her after Mike's death, but she'd noticed it each time they'd been close recently. Her pulse sped.

Noticing it now wasn't less scary.

And wanting him for this moment wasn't wrong. It didn't mean she'd come to rely on him or that he'd stay when it was all over. For now, for just a little while in the security of his embrace, she pretended she was special to him.

"Mags, I'm going to make this right."

She shook her head. "Things will never be right again."

"Ooh, honey." He rubbed his hands along her back and pressed her closer. "It feels that way now, but things will get better."

"You can clean up and scrub away the physical reminders of what's happened to my family, but the images live in my mind." Leaning away from him a little, she swiped her hands under her eyes. "I'll never completely get over the feeling of being violated."

"Good." His gentle eyes contradicted his harsh tone. "You don't get over what's happened, Mags."

"Very encouraging, Harte."

He smiled and traced his thumb along her cheek. "You don't get over it. You embrace it. You move past it. You let it make you stronger and smarter."

Let it make you stronger and smarter. Closing her eyes, she thought about his advice. She'd survived a year of single-motherhood and grief. She could survive this. She'd grown stronger during her pregnancy and dealing with the day-to-day details of being a widow and single mom.

Stronger. Smarter. Braver.

Breathing deep, she opened her eyes and rested a palm on his cheek. "You cleaned my house."

He lowered his gaze and shrugged. "It was no big deal."

"It is to me, and you know that. I'm losing my grip." Her grip on the control she'd fought for to survive was slowly eroding as if it was being worn like seashells on an ocean's shore.

"You've been faced with a lot in a few days. You'll be fine." He cradled her in his arms as if she weighed nothing and meant everything.

Resisting him grew tougher. Falling for him became a real possibility, and she was too vulnerable to deal with it when he left. Still, she craved the intimacy of the closeness they shared in these moments.

Before she could register what he was doing, he repositioned his arms with one behind her back and the other beneath her legs and picked her up. Letting herself enjoy this moment, she rested her head on his shoulder, inhaled his spicy scent and wrapped her arms around his neck. A sigh of happiness escaped, but she didn't care.

His strength seeped into her. Something bigger was coming, but she'd take a few more moments of peace. "Where are you taking me?"

"To take a bath."

Her eyes popped open. "H—"

"By yourself. You need to relax and forget about everything for awhile longer."

He stepped into her bathroom. Her mouth gaped at the scene he'd set. Lit pink and white candles lined her vanity and the sauna tub she so rarely got to use. The room smelled of her two favorite scents—vanilla and roses. The tub was full and the book she'd been reading in his room waited on the edge, beckoning her with promises of relaxation.

"You don't fight fair."

"*This* isn't a battle, Mags."

Maybe not, but they would have one before much longer. He sat her on her feet and walked over to her iPod dock. When he pushed play, the soulful melodies of Hans Zimmer floated into the room, bringing to mind an *almost* irresistible image.

Harte would pick her up and carry her to the high part of the vanity, and gently put her down. After a lingering, tender kiss, an exploration into the recesses of her mouth, he would lower to his knees and remove her shoes. Holding her gaze, his hands would travel up her legs and he'd unbutton her slacks before she'd lift up so he could slide her pants over her hips and down, until she sat before him in her blouse and panties.

Slowly, with passion darkening his eyes and the most tender of touches he would run his hands up her legs until he stood before her. His long, strong fingers would glide over her hips to the hem of her shirt and then over her sides as he eased it up her body and over her head.

Sitting before him in nothing more than her bra and thong, never breaking eye contact, she'd move her hands over his hard, rippling chest. The soft dusting of hair tickling her palms as she followed the narrowing trail down his stomach to the waist of his pants. She'd dip her fingers into the elastic and push them down.

"…be right back."

"What?" Maggie jerked herself away from her thoughts and looked at Harte. What had she missed? Fire raged through her veins, her system revved from the intensely intimate fantasy. A fantasy she *really* wanted to embrace, if only she thought she could handle it.

Swallowing the desire, hoping like hell she sounded fairly intelligent, she stepped forward. "Harte…"

He took her face in his big warm hands and smiled. "You need this."

"I…"

Cutting off any argument, he grasped her waist, lifted her off the floor and carried her to the vanity before he knelt and pulled her shoes and socks off.

Sucking in a breath, she waited.

Would he kiss her? Would her fantasy turn into reality? She wanted it to, but if it did, if he touched her as she'd pictured, if he kissed her, control would soar out the window. She'd lose her soul to him.

He sat her shoes neatly beside the vanity, stood and grabbed her waist to help her stand again. Disorientation and dizziness slammed into her before she realized she held air trapped in her lungs.

Keeping her gaze steady on his, she slowly exhaled and became aware of her tingling skin and damp panties. She didn't have a chance of holding out against any move he made. And while she wanted him to devour her, wanted to devour him in return, she needed him to go away.

She couldn't think with him so close, smelling spicy and hot with his half-naked, muscled body close enough to touch.

"You're too tense. Relax." He pressed a gentle kiss to her forehead and left the bathroom.

What? She'd missed something. She just couldn't think of what it might be, not that it mattered. He'd left. She had space, except his scent lingered. She gave in to her shaking knees and leaned against the counter. She'd thought for a second she would be lucky enough to have her fantasy. Her naked and sweaty fantasy.

"Snap out of it." Slapping her hands against her heated cheeks cleared her mind. A little. Enough that she could get undressed for her bath. Sex, no matter how tempting, wasn't happening.

She would take the opportunity he'd presented and enjoy the soft music, scented candles, and a long bath. Anything else would wait. Easing another button free, she assured herself she shouldn't feel guilty for anticipating the pleasure of no interruptions while she indulged in her own slice of Paradise.

"Oh hell."

With her fingers releasing the next button, she glanced up. Harte stood in the doorway with flames of awareness that sliced through her and relit the fire she'd barely begun to extinguish ablaze in his gaze.

Following his eyes, she looked down at her shirt gaping open to her belly button and the fire red, lace bra that echoed her thoughts.

Come and get me.

BD's eyes popped wide. The gentle swell of Maggie's breasts peeking over the take-me red bra begged for his touch. Her rigid nipples standing at attention pleaded for his mouth to suck on them, taste their honey. He nearly swallowed his tongue and barely withstood the desire to tip back the bottle of wine he held and chug it.

"Do you need something?" Her sultry whisper and the sight of the flush blooming over her flawless skin had the remaining blood in his head rushing south.

To spread you across the vanity and sample you like a buffet. To know if your panties are a thong matching your bra.

He lifted the wine and a glass. "I brought you this. I said I'd be right back." *Why the hell did you start undressing?*

"You... I..." She drew her lips together with a soft sucking sound, sealing her luscious mouth closed.

Her shirt still hung open. The pain of his swelling dick reminded him he was close to crossing a line he couldn't step back from. *Don't go there.*

"I'll just..." *Get the hell out. Now!* He sat the wine on the counter and stepped back, pointing over his shoulder to the door. "Um... I'll..."

He backed toward the door. She stepped forward, tongue

poking between the corner of her lips. The urge to bury himself in her, to lose himself in the pleasure without thought of the consequences sizzled in his veins. *The job comes first. Involvement is dangerous.*

Like a spineless coward, he moved fast across the house. The more distance he put between him and her, the less likely he was to find out how perfectly her breasts would fit in his hands. He started to detour to the kitchen for a beer, but under the circumstances one would lead to two...he needed a clear head. Not that the image of rose petal soft skin and red lace indelibly lodged in his brain made clarity an immediate possibility. Or a distant one.

He walked the house, searched the living room bookshelves for anything of potential interest for Adalia, and checked all the locks before getting his laptop from the kitchen and going back to his room.

All the while his skin vibrated with the knowledge of Maggie submerged in warm, frothy water. Naked.

Pinching his nose did nothing to ease the pressure of the images pushing against his mind or make focusing on work easier.

Pulling a metal box from beneath his bed, he took out copies of Adalia's files and the notes she'd left at each scene. Something tied the murders and Maggie together. More accurately something tied the previous murders and whatever papers Mike had had together. The clue had to be in the notes.

Pen and paper in hand, he spread the notes out on the floor in the order they'd been left and began analyzing them. Separately, together or shifted around, he would find whatever answer they held. He would discover the links.

Alicia Daniels, victim one. BD jotted notes on the pad. She'd been an investment adviser. Known as a young shark in a competitive business. Several people in her field had fought for her client list after her death. Her note had been left in an open wall safe.

"Venerated among Greek Gods, they knew true power."

It stood to reason Adalia had taken money or bonds from the safe. Nothing had turned up to prove the theory, but she'd have money stashed.

Victim number two was found a week later. A retired cartographer, Brent Porter had led a solitary life since his wife's passing a few months before his murder. The note had been pinned to his naked, half-mutilated body like a nametag.

"They hid the black conductor, but the guardian will not keep it from me."

Presumably, *they* referred to whomever Adalia spoke of in her first note. The trouble was knowing who they were and what the black conductor was. The guardian part was obvious. Someone was protecting whatever she wanted. Maybe that's how she chose her victims. Maybe they all had something to do with the conductor she was after.

An archeology professor at the University of Texas at Dallas had been the third victim. Simon Hodges, an intellectual, bow-tie type who'd reportedly buried himself in books when he wasn't at dig sites.

"Burdensome buried relics live through history. I know who has the answers."

Professor at UT. He should have seen it before. That had to be where the connection to Mike began. The men had taught at the same school. It wasn't too much of a stretch to believe they would collaborate on something like ancient papers. Some relics were believed to have powers, control curses or a ton of other nonsense. Burying them wouldn't erase their legends or histories, but it could vanish or diminish the power.

If Adalia was after an actual relic, was it for a power she thought was hidden or something else entirely? Money?

There had been no note for Mike's death, so they had thought the connection was more personal. Without him, the other notes hadn't made sense. Now, taking them all in a new context, there had to be a common tie to whatever ancient papers Mike had seemingly been translating. Discovery was their only hope to learning why Adalia wanted the papers.

But why Michelle Dane? She hadn't been at the university while Mike was there, which meant she wouldn't likely know about the papers.

BD pulled out crime scene photos of each victim and placed them above the notes side-by-side.

Michelle Dane's photo sat beside the archeology professor. They had both worked at UT, had collaborated on a few projects, but there was another connection.

"No way." He flipped through her file and skimmed notes from interviews before he grabbed his phone and dialed. Craig picked up on the second ring.

"Yeah."

"Michelle Dane. What do we know about her family history?"

Craig sighed, clearly holding back an announcement of what time it was. "She was an only child. Adopted. Never married."

"We need to confirm it," BD tapped the two pictures holding his interest. "But I'm pretty sure I just found her bioligical father."

He wrapped up with Craig and made more notes on his pad. It couldn't be coincidental that she'd been in the same field as her birth father, worked at the same university, and had been killed by the same woman.

"You'll not stop me this time, but you can have a chance to save those under your protection. Your failure will result in mass destruction."

The note left on Michelle Dane had been directed at BD

and Craig and had served as a threat to Maggie, though she'd been targeted more because of her connection to the late archeologist and by extension Mike.

Studying the latest notes, BD looked for more links.

"The cops will not get in the middle again. I'll have the key to harnessing the power."

"Mike paid for turning me in. Don't try to outsmart me. Get me the papers or die."

Out of context they seemed as random as the murder victims, which now seemed anything but random. The underlying tone in the notes dealt with history. Each victim had been a specialist in their field. Mike Sullivan had been an ancient languages expert and a seemingly upstanding guy. The only one who didn't fit with ancient papers was the investment broker.

Opening his laptop, BD pulled up Google and tried different search parameters hoping to whittle away at the endless possibilities. Once they figured out what the papers were about they could set a trap. And he'd make sure they snared Adalia's accomplice too.

When the pages blurred, BD rubbed his hands over his face. Whoever said being a cop was exciting didn't realize how tedious and mind-numbing it could be, though not numbing enough to fully dislodge the persistent impressions Maggie left in her wake.

Even now, her scent invaded his thoughts, made him remember her taste and revived the hum of arousal he'd been battling since moving in. If things went too far, and they easily could, she would own his soul.

He couldn't risk Maggie because of lust and stupidity. Her children would not be made orphans. Another woman would not die because of him.

"You're going to be stooped over like an old man if you

spend much more time on the floor hunched over papers and your laptop."

He jerked and spun to face Maggie. His mind whirled with possible ways of keeping her from seeing the content of the papers all around, yet a quick look at her and thoughts of papers vanished. She was a sucker punch to the groin.

Standing just outside his door, looking firmly in control again, she wore a neon blue, satin tank top that hugged the curves of her unbound breasts. Form-fitting workout shorts not much bigger than the boy-short style underwear some women wore drew his attention to her legs. He wondered which thong she had on under the shorts. Unless she didn't have any on.

His cock saluted the commando idea.

Damn it. Where were the baggy pajama pants she'd worn last night? Her current get up made it all too easy to recall the softness of her shape beneath him. Her hair hung, unbraided, almost to her waist in magnificent damp waves. Some of the wetness had moistened her top and now showcased stiff nipples.

With Herculean effort, he casually began gathering the notes. "Are you hungry?"

"Not really." She leaned against the door and crossed her arms over the bright top, pushing her breasts up until their swells peeked out. Humor curled her lip subtly, just as Sam's had done when she watched him work.

The base of his back itched with memories and stirring desires. He looked back to the floor and papers. "Right."

The home and family he'd always wanted had been his for a few brief months. Now, he had to remember it was gone. Maggie wasn't a replacement. He wouldn't take chances again. The price was unaffordable.

"Have you had any luck figuring out what Adalia's after?"

BD evaluated his options of how much to tell her, and how to break his latest news. Picking up the papers and laptop, he moved to his desk. "Still working on it."

"Are the papers you're hiding helping?"

Damn woman was too perceptive. "Not really."

"So, nothing new." She walked over and sat on the end of the bed. "What do we do now?"

He averted his eyes from her lean legs as he turned the chair and straddled it. She pulled her legs up to sit Indian style. The sinew of her slender thighs flexed slightly. He lost track of the conversation. Just how flexible was she? How adventurous would she be in bed?

"Harte."

He blinked and forced his mind back to a safer path. "Yeah?"

"What happens next? Do you have any idea how you're going to catch her?"

"We have some leads. Until we...validate them—"

"They mean nothing."

The pulse pounded against the tender skin of her neck. From fear? Arousal? "You don't want to know the things I know about Adalia. I wouldn't tell you if you did."

Maggie closed her eyes and took a few steady breaths before looking at him again. "When are you going to tell me anything?"

The woman's control astounded him. Considering the mental hits she'd taken, she was holding up really well. And she'd voluntarily sent her kids away. That couldn't have been easy.

"Consider it need to know." The less she knew the better. He'd never talk to anyone other than Craig about the details of the job again. As for Maggie, he wanted to shelter her from the pain of knowing her husband may have been connected to Adalia.

Feeling like a caged animal, BD lurched off the chair and paced the room. Craig had a freakish control that kept him cool-headed at all times. BD couldn't make such a claim. Another reason he was the wrong guy to be guarding her. First thing in the morning he was switching places with Craig.

"Harte, sit."

Quirking a brow, he slowly pivoted on his heel. She had *not* just commanded him like she might a dog. "Excuse me?"

"Sit." Oooh, the I'm-a-mother-and-will-be-obeyed-tone grated. She'd found an exposed nerve and was virtually digging her finger in it. Obeying her order was the last thing he would do.

He watched her and crossed his arms. "You sound amazingly as if you're commanding a mutt."

"No." Maggie straightened her spine so stiff she could have passed for an aristocrat thumbing her nose at him. "More like a stubborn man who thinks he's doing me a favor by not telling me what he knows."

"Mags…"

"Don't 'Mags' me."

He clenched his jaw and breathed slowly, trying to see past the red haze in front of him. He stalked toward the end of the bed, bearing down on her.

She fell backward, bracing herself on her elbows. Her legs dropped off the bed, but her gaze never wavered. "I want answers. It was one thing to keep secrets before Adalia walked into my home. Before uprooting my kids became a necessity. Before my home was vandalized and bugged. I *deserve* to know what's going on."

BD stood between her slightly spread legs, crossed his arms behind his back, and bending at the waist, leaned in. "You don't want the answers I have."

"You're not doing me any favors by keeping secrets." Her sexy voice carried as much power and conviction as if she'd been standing toe-to-toe with him.

Even half-reclining on the end of his bed, with her legs straddling his in a potentially sexual position, she jutted her stubborn chin out in defiance. Yeah, she'd recovered from her meltdown and she was sticking to her guns.

Irresistible.

"Damn it, speak." The bark of her command busted the first snap on his control.

His blood raged. BD swooped down. She jerked her head backward an inch. Bracing his arms on the bed at the sides of her hips, he lowered himself until his nose brushed hers, leaving her no option but to lay all the way back if she wanted to avoid touching him.

She dropped flat. He grinned.

"Believe me." Straining against the invisible leash holding his temper and desire in check, the words ground from between clenched teeth. "You want some of the favors I'm granting."

"No!"

If she'd intended to say anything else he didn't care. He captured her luscious, protesting mouth and poured every ounce of anger and aggression and passion swirling in his veins into the kiss. Restraining himself from doing more, knowing possessing her would only make matters worse, he maintained the minimal distance between their bodies. Still, he angled his head and explored her open mouth.

She tasted like the honey he'd imagined earlier when she faced him in her red lace bra. Under the sweetness was a hint of spice. The same spice he'd tasted every other time he'd kissed her. If he continued, her body would heat up. She'd be moaning, and he would take her all the way with him.

Jerking away from the temptation threatening his sanity, he left her sprawled on his bed, and stalked to the window to look through the narrowly cracked blinds.

"Harte—"

Knowing if he looked at her he would see flushed cheeks and dilated pupils, he kept his back to the room. "Don't push me, Mags. You aren't ready for the consequences."

"You—"

"Here's the deal." Spinning to face her, he found her sitting with her back ramrod straight. Regal as royalty, she stood and braced her hands at the indention of her waist. Her slender fingers, gifted with the ability to incite fires in his body, tapped her pelvis.

He slid his gaze down her sexy, toned legs to her red

toenails—God what was it with her and that color—and slowly back up. The fire in her eyes warned him to keep a safe distance between them. She looked violent, aroused and he'd seen what she could do with those lethal legs and a well-placed kick.

Collecting what little control he still possessed, he walked over and leaned against the desk. She wanted to know things? So did he.

"Adalia takes grotesque pleasure in tormenting her victims." He may be a bastard, but she'd asked for it. "She's been in your home twice. Whoever is helping her has the resources of the Dallas Police at his disposal and, unless I'm wrong, he's watching you when she isn't. You can tell yourself this is all because of me, but reality is different. And Adalia is only giving you a small taste of the tricks in her arsenal.

"Brace yourself, sugar," he plundered ahead. This was where it would get dicey. "Things are about to change."

"Excuse me?" She stalked toward him.

"You heard me." He mirrored her moves until they were in the middle of the floor.

Toe-to-toe.

Nose-to-nose.

Aggression-to-aggression.

"We are dealing with a woman capable of doing things most men wouldn't dream of. If she hadn't passed psychiatric tests I'd argue she's not entirely sane. Either way, things are changing. Now."

Her eyes widened and she pursed her mouth, obviously thinking of her next move. In this, he was focused. Nothing would derail him.

"By 'things' you think you're going to boss me around and I'm going to blindly follow?"

"I *know* you *will* do certain things my way." He raised a brow daring her to argue. "Others are open to minor negotiations."

"Hah!"

"Scoff all you want." Reveling in the odd sensation of being in complete, cool control of himself for the first time since stepping into her house, BD eased his chest down until he brushed against hers. "I'm serious."

A droning silence passed with them staring each other down, neither willing to back down. She played this game with her kid. BD played it with killers.

"Tell me what you *think* is going to happen."

He grinned. He would've won in the end, but at least this way maybe it could be handled with less arguing. "For starters, we will be sleeping in the same room until this is done. Yours or mine, it's your pick, but we will be sharing a room."

"I will not!" Shaking her head, she backed away.

He snaked a hand out, grabbed her wrist and yanked her back to him. Pinning her body to his, he shook his head. "This is *not* one of the negotiable points. Until this is over you don't leave my sight."

"I'd like to see you try to enforce that."

In a blink, BD picked her up and sent her flying through the air. She landed on the mattress with an inelegant grunt. She didn't even bounce and he was on top of her. He pressed his body against hers, inch for inch, and made himself deadweight.

She grunted, wiggled, pushed at his sides, wiggled again. Then she pounded on his back. Jockeying for a more comfortable position, and safer should she start in with her knees, he wedged his knees between hers.

Using her new freedom, she lifted her legs and kicked him wherever her feet could reach. His cock hardened, begging for a role in the fight. Calling himself a bastard for the immense pleasure and arousal he got out of the situation, he nuzzled into her neck.

The scent of vanilla and roses clung to her skin and hair from her bath. Lowering his lids so they were barely open, he inhaled, drew her essence inside himself. It only enhanced his discomfort—physical and emotional. She tangled him up, made him want things he'd given up on.

He couldn't give in to the temptation. This was a war for her life.

He slid his hands up her legs and over her hips. The tight shorts left little to the imagination, but the absence of a panty line had him wondering again if she wore a thong or nothing at all.

She continued to writhe and kick and when none of that budged him, she wrapped her fantastic legs around his waist and bucked her hips. Despite the razor of pleasure shooting up his spine and filling his gut, he laughed against her ear.

"You can fight all night, Mags. You're not getting out of this arrangement."

"Jerk." She didn't need to yell for him to feel her vehemence.

"I know." To prove his point, he nipped at her ear.

"You can't force me to sleep with you." That she turned his statement about sharing a room into them sharing a bed was proof she wanted him. He wasn't going to argue the point.

Slipping his hands beneath her, he cupped her backside and pulled her against him, making it clear what else he'd like to do tonight. He traced the crown of her ear with his tongue. "One way or the other."

"I'm not having sex with you."

The soft, sensual Maggie had a spine of steel, but there were limits to her resolve. He would take advantage of them if need be. And hope he survived.

"You can't resist me forever." Pressing his hips into hers, cursing the layers of clothes separating them, he waited until she huffed out a breath and stopped squirming. "But perhaps you'll want option number two."

"Doubtful."

He raised his head enough to meet her gaze. Golden sparks of passion and anger flashed in her brown depths. *Magnificent.*

"I've already seen most of the delights you have to offer." Torn between rage and unmistaken ardor, she turned his body into an inferno. Lifting a brow, he reached for the hem of her tank top and inched the fabric up almost daring her not to protest. "Want me to see the rest? 'Cause I'm game."

"Get off me." She bucked against him once more.

"Not yet."

She screamed at the top of her lungs and hit and kicked him with everything she had. He got close to her ear again.

"Hit, kick, scream," he whispered. She heard him despite her screams. "You feel what you're doing to me. We both know you aren't afraid."

Her body went instantly limp.

"Mags." BD watched a lone tear trip down her cheek and felt like a slug, but it didn't change what he needed to do. "I'm not going to do anything you don't ask me to do. Sexually, anyway. Got it?"

She nodded and steadily met his gaze.

"You want to hear the other option?"

She swallowed and nodded again.

"I thought you might." Watching for signs of violence, he sat up between her legs and reached into his pocket.

She pushed up to her elbows, her legs still stretched along either side of him. "What's that?"

"A full night's sleep in a pill." *At least for one of us.*

"You're going to drug me?"

He shook his head. As much as he'd like to force her to take the pill, for his own peace of mind, he had to let it be her choice. "It's your prescription. I found it in the kitchen. Very mild, but under the circumstances, I think you could use a full eight hours."

"I don't like taking them. They leave me feeling loopy in the morning. What's my other option?"

"You can have an extremely restless night knowing I'm inches away from you." He invaded her space again to make sure she got the point. "Aroused… Ready."

She scrambled back and knelt on the edge of the bed. He fully expected her to tell him where to shove the sleeping pill and his plans for the night's arrangements.

"I'll take the pill." She held her hand out, palm up. "And I'm sleeping in my bedroom."

He placed the pill in her palm, but grabbed her hand tight when she started to pull back. Her eyes flared. "You *can* trust me, Mags."

"You, yes. What you make me want, no."

Chapter Nine

BD watched Maggie sleep from the chair in the corner. At least half an hour had passed with him telling himself he was making sure she wasn't going to wake. In reality, he wanted to study her when she wasn't cleaning or cooking or dealing with the kids or working at her computer. The woman went constantly.

She'd pulled a pillow against her chest and curled into it, snugging it against her supple curves so sweetly he imagined himself as the pillow. Her mouth smiled gently and her scent floated through the room. More than when he'd held her a year earlier, more than when he'd held her before taking her to the bath, she was completely vulnerable.

He craved the privilege to curl beside her, to hold her, to make her his. But she was taboo.

She stretched in an unconscious search for more comfort. The pill had done its job and pulled her into a deep sleep, yet her quiet breaths sending her luscious breasts up and down gave him little hope for a mental disconnect.

She represented everything he had wanted from life. He should have traded places with Craig. Instead he'd kept his decision to himself, stayed and struggled to remember his stance on relationships. Everything about this woman screamed "commit".

She was everything he thirsted and hungered for. And everything he avoided.

Closing his laptop, he rose and walked to the bed to pull the blanket over her. Her hand jerked on the pillow. Wondering if the sleeping pill was wearing off, BD watched her closely. Her eyes twitched rapidly beneath closed lids.

She stiffened and shook her head. "No! He... I..."

Pain and sadness darkened her voice, tugged at the corner of his heart he needed to guard. The shackles shook and his desire to be a man not a cop surged forth—the way it always did with her.

BD brushed a hand along her arm to offer comfort as much as to satisfy his need to touch. She sighed. Her body melted into the mattress.

"Mmm, you're back." Her voice went from frantic to happy in seconds.

Back? Seeing his hand against her skin, tasting the temptation to bulldoze boundaries, he pulled away. As much as he wanted to know the pleasure of her touch, he would not risk his focus and her safety.

Keeping a close watch, he backed toward the door. Maggie slept on peacefully, secure in her home which was typically full of love and people who mattered. Momentarily weak in the knees, he leaned against the doorframe and struggled to catch his breath.

Closing the bedroom door behind him, locking away his emotions, BD forced his mind into work mode and mentally shifted through the hints Adalia had left. Somewhere in Maggie's life and Adalia's notes were answers. Now, with Maggie asleep, he would search everything in the house until he found it.

Walking past the pictures of her family covering the hallway walls, which made it obvious how comfortable and happy they'd been, he admitted to himself how solidly she and her kids had wrapped him around their fingers in a matter of days. Emma with her blue eyes and innocence. Jared with his wounded spirit and eager mind. The kids belonged to the man in a photo sitting close to Maggie on a wooden bench beneath a huge tree, but BD missed them. Cared for them. Hell, he loved them.

He was living in Maggie's home, but would never be hers. They'd captivated him without his awareness. If she knew what he suspected, she would kick him to the curb harder than she kicked her punching bag. Searching her home was a betrayal of her trust, and she'd made it clear how she felt on that subject, but he had no choice. He needed to know her husband's level of involvement.

Stopping in the kitchen, he set a pot of coffee to brew in hopes it would burn away a few cobwebs. He'd searched the cupboards and undersides of the drawers while she'd taken the kids to her parents.

If Mike had hidden the papers in the house, he'd have picked an easily accessible, secure and unexpected spot. Coffee cup in hand, BD checked the picture frames on the hallway walls before he searched the hutch and underside of the dining room table and checked inside planters to make sure they held nothing but plants. In the living room, he flipped the couch and chairs over and felt along the undersides and the back of the entertainment center. He unzipped cushion covers and checked inside the sofa lining.

The search would go faster if he didn't take the time to put things back precisely as he'd found them. Well, most everything. He left her knick-knacks and throw pillows slightly askew.

Coming up empty handed in yet another room, he headed for the office. He and Craig had been looking for something left behind by Adalia when they searched it. Now, he searched the files more thoroughly and looked between the pages of every book on the shelves for hidden papers. Or anything Mike might have left behind.

Finding nothing, he moved to the computer. The rising sun was beginning to peek through the closed blinds. Time was running out before Maggie would wake.

Settled at her desk, BD turned on the computer and fished through the desk drawers again.

Looking at a picture of Jared and his dad on the same bench as several other pictures, he wondered if it had been taken at the farm. It was obviously a favorite spot for them.

Turning his attention to the quietly humming computer, he browsed through her documents and folders. The woman had file folders within file folders within file folders. Under

Ancestry, there were two folders. Sullivan and Malone. Double clicking on Sullivan he found a folder for Phil, Betty and Mike.

He double clicked Mike and found more folders. Anything he could want to know about Mike seemed to be there: Birth, Dreams, Health, Friends, Goals, Growth, Hobbies, Jobs, School, Sports, Studies.

He double clicked jobs. The twenty-two inch screen filled with more folders. "Good grief."

Scrolling through them, he found one Word document not in a file: Simon Says. Simon Hodges had been one of Adalia's victims. Raising his eyebrows, BD double clicked the icon to open the document.

Simon claims that while he is unsure of their origin, the scrolls are three-thousand years old. I am unsure of how they came to him, but am intrigued and excited to delve into the Hyperborean language as it's one I've seen only once before.

Update: I have only begun translating the Hyperborean scrolls onto paper. I don't know what these people discovered, but what I've garnered so far is worrisome. I tried to consult with Simon. His curiosity seems to have been replaced by hesitancy and fear.

Update: Simon has been killed. I cannot help but wonder if it was because of the scrolls. I also wonder if I am now in danger. I have been contacted by a woman claiming to be a student interested in ancient languages, specifically Hyperboreans. I will meet with her, but am suspicious about the timing of her contact. It is too coincidental.

Before our meeting, I will put the scrolls where security is as commonplace as peace. Should Simon's death be related to the papers, should I meet a similar end, I will see that Maggie and Jared are safe.

BD checked the document's history to get a timeline for

the updates and tried to place where he'd heard of the Hyperboreans. The memory eluded him, so he focused on facts.

Simon's murder was one week after he'd given Mike the scrolls, not papers apparently. Mike's mention of the pending appointment had been another week later—the day before his death. Whatever he'd learned at that meeting, whatever he had found that had motivated him to report Adalia, would remain a mystery. The notes did absolve him of any shady connections to Adalia.

"What are you doing?"

BD jumped, smacked his knee on the corner of the desk. Swallowing an insane lump of guilt, and struggling to think past his slamming heart, he closed the file and turned to face Maggie. *Damn.* The word drawled long and dramatic in his head.

Like the night before, she stood in the doorway with her arms crossed over her chest. Her breasts swelled up over the top of her tank. Her hair was mussed from sleep, but her eyes were sharp and snapping with anger. So much for the drugs making her fuzzy the next morning.

He needed an excuse. Fast.

"Using the computer." *Unoriginal, but absolutely true.*

"Something wrong with yours?" She looked sexy as hell all mussed up from sleep. A line creased her cheek where her face had pressed into the sheets.

"Battery needs charged."

She shook her head. "Plug it in."

"Forgot the power cord at the station."

"Get an extra one."

He had an extra, but she didn't need to know that. "Will do."

"Right. Listen…" Her suspicion seemed to ease off though it didn't go away entirely. "Thanks for last night. I'm going to get dressed. I have things to do."

She tacked on the last bit as if saying thanks made her

uncomfortable. Unless her discomfort came from other memories.

He shifted a little to ease the pressure building at the base of his spine. His cell phone rang and he pulled it from his pocket. When he saw Craig's number, he flipped it open. He smiled at Maggie and waited for her to be well out of earshot.

"Give me good news." He ignored the edge of desperation in his voice. He didn't honestly expect Craig to have solved the case over night on his own.

"Sorry, man. I'm not finding anything. I played with the parameters of the Google searches, but still haven't found anything to make sense." Craig rambled about the different things he'd found and negated. "You have any luck?"

"Maybe." BD moved into the hall and told Craig about Mike's notes. He wanted to minimize any chance of Maggie hearing him, but he also needed to stay watchful over her.

"Old scrolls written by Hyperboreans that have been hidden. So helpful." Craig blew out a frustrated breath. "This is going to take longer to solve than we have. Adalia won't stay hidden long."

BD checked his watch. Two more minutes and he was going in.

"I know a way." The door opened and Maggie sailed out of her room in a pair of jeans and an outrageous pink T-shirt, barely sparing a glance for him as she went toward the kitchen. BD followed Maggie's path, enjoying the curve of her hips and ass showcased in the snug, low-riding jeans. "But I don't like it."

"You going to ask her about Mike?"

It could help. "Apparently." In a moment of perversity, BD rearranged the pillows on the couch again. "Maybe he mentioned the Hyperboreans to her. Maybe she's at least seen these ancient scrolls—"

"Shit." Craig interrupted. "I've got it." His typically modulated tone grew excited.

"What?"

"You remember the trip to the Arctic we took with my parents?"

"We were kids. What about it?" They'd been thirteen and had sworn they would freeze before they saw fourteen.

"They found proof of an ancient people who dated back three-thousand years. Later they said they thought they might have been the Hyperboreans. Maybe they were a real civilization."

A finger snap in BD's brain brought the memory and Craig's parents' suppositions back. "Ancient scrolls proving the existence of ancient people believed to socialize with Greek gods would be worth a ton of money."

"Yeah." Craig cleared his throat. "Go easy on her, BD."

"I have been."

"You haven't."

"Piss off."

"You have the hots for her and it scares the shit out of you," Craig continued with a hint of know-it-all attitude. "You're trying not to see her as a woman because you don't want to risk getting hurt again, but you could be the one doing the hurting."

"I said piss off, Oprah." *He isn't so wrong though.* The backdoor slammed. Adrenaline sped through BD's veins as he clutched the phone tight and sprinted into the kitchen in time to see Maggie cross the lawn.

Did he really have to spell it out for her that she was in danger? Did she have to make herself an easy target? Tapping the hedge clippers against her leg, Maggie faced the bushes she'd attacked the other day. At least she was armed.

She cocked her head to the left and then the right as if judging where to pick up what she'd barely started. Her hair, again in a braid, swayed with her movements. His fingers itched to loosen it and feel the thick silk tangled in his fingers.

"BD." Craig's voice snapped him back. "Get it through your skull. She isn't Samantha. Talk to Maggie and let me know what she tells you."

Craig hung up, leaving BD to dwell on his parting. Maggie really was nothing like Sam had been, and he'd do a better job protecting her.

He couldn't wish his feelings away or lie to himself. He cared for Maggie and hated the idea of questioning her husband's associations. Worse, he hated thinking about what Adalia would do to her.

Harte's secrets were growing bigger. He'd had her take the sleeping pill so he could search her house. What did he think he'd find? What did he suspect her of?

The secrets, lies and omissions were closing in on her like walls on a claustrophobe. The suffocating air in her own home was tainted with betrayal. She'd had enough of having her opinions minimized in her marriage.

Fueled by building anger, Maggie faced the detestable bushes and shivered at the sensation of teeny little critters crawling across her skin. Lifting the clippers, putting every ounce of frustration flooding her veins into the effort, she chopped off the closest branch. Hacking away at the eyesores, feeling stronger and more in control of her own destiny, she grinned.

No more doing what other people wanted—including Harte. No more smothering, protective, I-know-what's-best attitudes. Who did he think he was?

Tossing branches blindly behind her, she attacked the next section. No matter how sexy the man was, his caveman behavior wasn't appealing—except for the perverse pleasure of being pinned beneath him and that was acceptable.

Her heart raced. The branches snapped easily beneath the pressure of the cutter blades. Each snapping branch echoed another snapping restraint she'd put on herself for years.

She grabbed more branches and tossed them in the general direction of the pile she had going. Then she went after a fatter bough, cutting close to the ground. Her clippers barely scored its thickness. Frustrating, but not surprising considering the age and health of the monstrosity.

After making another score, she lowered the clippers to her side, angled her body so she stood parallel to the bush, and put every ounce of frustration behind the kick she aimed at the branch. Like a rubber band on a slingshot, the thing wobbled and sprang back into place. Jumping back to keep from getting hit, she glared at the offending limb.

It had to go, and Harte's chauvinism could go with it. The man had nerve. Telling her she couldn't go anywhere, saying he'd sleep in her room, and then blowing her off to take a phone call.

She would inform him that no matter what the circumstances may be, he would not be sleeping in her room uninvited. And no way was she inviting him. Even the sleeping pill failed to sufficiently blur the night before and her responses to him. Her body heated again just thinking about his blatant arousal pressed against her.

Maggie arched her back to dislodge the pool of sweat forming. He tempted her, whether he was near her or not. Last night, he'd been very near. So near she'd been close to taking advantage of his body.

She stepped on the un-breaking branch, managing to bend it just a little, and took the choppers to it again. Several cuts and screaming muscles later, the thing snapped loose with a loud pop. The cracking release of the branch reverberated through her.

Her foot slipped off the branch. Off balance, she stumbled backwards a few steps before regaining her balance. The mass of anger and pent up arousal swirling through her gut gushed out leaving her unusually exhausted.

"You keep working like that and you're going to do more than scrape a knee."

She spun around and faced Harte. "I can take care of myself."

"Good." He leaned against the picnic table with his arms

and legs crossed. "I'm not sure my first aid would be as gentle or memorable as yours."

The reminder of her tending to his hand slammed into her brain. More prevalent, though, was the image of him completely nude and aroused when he'd dropped the towel. *Don't go there.*

Blinking the thoughts away, she studied him. He appeared calm and relaxed. *It's an act.*

The muscle in his jaw ticked. His eyes, generally cobalt, had darkened to the point that if she wanted to see where his iris met his pupil they would have to be standing toe-to-toe.

The nuances of his movements, like the twitching of his thumb, said he was angry, though nothing broadcast the message as blatantly as the heat of restrained rage radiating off him. Any closer and it would singe her.

"We need to talk."

"Yes. We do." She jabbed the blades into the ground and walked around the giant pile of bush clippings to the picnic table. If he wanted to play this cool then she would try to accommodate. But his eyes, now midnight blue and tracking every move she made, had her nerves humming with fear and doubt.

She worked her wedding ring in circles as she sat on the top of the table. He turned and sat beside her with his feet on the bench seat. She felt the low level hum of arousal only he seemed to cause, but for once it didn't overshadow everything else.

His anxiety made her fidgety. She slid her ring on and off, almost dropping it once. Her feet tapped the table.

"Maggie."

Maggie. Not Mags. He always shortened her name unless they were arguing or he had bad news. "What's wrong now?"

"We need to talk."

"So you said." He had to be desperate to be coming to her. "Is this where you tell me what you've been holding back?"

"If I could keep this from hurting I would."

She stiffened her posture and narrowed her eyes. What could be worse than him telling her Mike was dead and she'd been targeted by a killer? "Spit it out."

"Mike's death was... He was killed so he wouldn't talk. And I think because Adalia felt he had betrayed her."

Every synapse in her brain fired. Her head tingled with awareness, but she would not fall apart. She had control. "What?"

"Mags."

"No." *Now he wants to personalize this?* "Tell me."

"You know about Adalia's past actiins."

"I was at some of her trial."

"Michelle Dane was a warning."

What he might say next weighed in her gut like a ton of lead. What did this have to do with Mike? Her? "How?"

"As well as being Mike's replacement at work, she was the daughter of another victim." Harte held her gaze. "A victim Mike consulted with on some scrolls before his death."

"You are saying Mike was involved with Adalia. That they were close enough for her to trust him and be angered by him."

BD sighed. His shoulders fell. Shaking his head, he maneuvered around to sit beside her. He braced his elbows on his knees and tapped his fingertips together. "I need you to tell me about Mike."

She stopped fiddling with her ring long enough to rub her throat. She wasn't wearing a necklace, but she had the strange sensation something was choking her. "Like what? He was a linguistics professor. That's not exciting stuff."

"Did he act any differently the weeks before his death? Did he mention a project or academic find he was excited about? Did you suspect him of cheating or having secrets?"

"No."

"Maggie."

Maggie again. Suddenly last night, his insistence on sleeping arrangements, and his now subdued attitude made more sense. It hadn't all been about Adalia's threats. They had information that pointed to Mike.

"No. No more evasions or omissions."

He dropped his head into his hands. "I don't like this."

"Join the club." She didn't want to hear it, but ignorance was more of a hindrance than bliss.

He looked up, watching her in a silent battle of wills before he reluctantly nodded. "You have to trust me to do what's right."

The message couldn't be any clearer that he didn't want her involved, but he was agreeing to open up—a privilege he doubtfully afforded to many people. She had nothing to hide, and would tell him whatever she could to clear Mike's name.

"What do you need to know?"

"Had he said anything about an ancient people or their language? Specifically Hyperboreans?"

"The picture in Jared's room is supposed to be of Hyperborea." She rubbed her temples. "They did it together. Mike made the place sound like fiction."

Harte told her about the notes Adalia had left and how he was coming to believe she was on the hunt for information. Anyone who knew too much got killed. Then he told her about Mike's note he'd found on her computer.

"Wait." She grabbed his arm. "He hid the scrolls where security is as commonplace as peace? Is that how he worded it?"

"Yeah." He straightened. "You know where he means?"

"Yes." She kissed him and jumped off the table. "We need to go for a ride. We're going to see my dad." *And my kids.*

Without waiting to make sure he kept up, she headed to the car.

Chapter Ten

Rounding a curve, the green pipe fence that stretched nearly a mile came into view. Directly in the middle of the fence line was a set of ornate iron gates with upside down horseshoes for catching good luck along the top. The superstition came from Mike's mom, Betty, but their families had both been lucky. No matter what threat had faced them over the years, they stood strong and prevailed.

"You grew up here?"

"Yeah." She took the split in the drive to the right and pulled up in front of the enormous barn. Meticulous flowerbeds, Betty's pride and joy, ran the length of the white, metal-sided building with a green roof. Several horses hung their heads out oversize windows.

"You must have loved it." Awe rode his smiling tone. "No wonder you seem more at home in your jeans and T-shirt than the slacks and blouses you've been wearing."

Her throat thickened. She was more a jeans and T-shirt kind of girl, but she didn't want to know what else he'd noticed about her. "Nothing quite like afternoons, weekends and summers mucking stalls, grooming horses, cleaning tack and doing uncountable other chores."

"Maybe." He turned and watched her as she put the Tahoe in park. "But what a place to go when life gets too crazy. To hide your kids from the chaos. To hide with them."

She turned the engine off and met his gaze. "Let me be crystal clear, Harte. I am *not* staying here."

"Mags."

"No." Shaking her head in exhausted frustration, she chose her words carefully because she didn't want to fight. "I get it. Adalia's dangerous. Protect me, but don't ask me to be a coward."

His fingertip caressed the barrel of his gun that he'd put

beside him on the seat. "I'd rather know you were safe out here."

"I *need* to face this head-on, or I'm not going to be able to look myself in the mirror."

He opened his mouth then snapped it shut and glared. His shoulders dropped and she knew she'd scored a point. He tried to be abrasive and insensitive but was an insightful and surprisingly sweet man. He could yell and scream the roof down, yet had a knack for easing her grief and fear.

She respected him and enjoyed spending time with him even with their current situation. Too bad.

She'd had no choice in losing Mike, but she'd realized after awhile she'd taken the safe move, gone for what she knew, settled. She would never settle again. She would be true to herself, and if a man came into the picture, he would have to view her as an equal partner. Harte couldn't be that man for her. Maybe for someone who could tolerate his need to be the alpha in all things or handle the possibility of losing him to his job. She however couldn't take the risk—no matter how closely he fit her desires.

Clearing the lump of depression in her throat she forced a smile. "Argue later. My family's waiting."

She moved away and hopped out of the Tahoe. He tucked his gun in his waistband and pulled his shirttail out as they approached the barn.

The faint smells of sweaty horses, just cleaned leather, freshly dumped manure, and the stink of fly spray welcomed her as she stepped into the barn offices. She pushed an inner door open in time to hear Jared pleading a very serious case to her mother.

"Grandma Di, tell Mom to let me have a puppy. She has to do what you tell her. You're the mom."

"Maybe you can try asking her very nicely." Her smile was patient and understanding as she pulled a fat black and white puppy from Jared's arms. "She's right behind you. Tell her hi and then go get your horse ready."

Jared spun around. His face split into a blinding grin, the first Maggie had seen since Mike's death, as he bounced on his feet to her and Harte. "Mom! Can I have a puppy? Please. Burke! Are you gonna watch me ride?"

Oh God. Maggie's heart lurched. Restrained tears lodged in her throat. Her hand shook as she rested it on her son's smiling face and unable to speak, she nodded.

Harte glanced between them before he ruffled Jared's hair and knelt. "I'd love to see you ride. First, tell me which puppy you're going to pick."

Maggie swiped at her eyes and looked away from Jared and Harte huddled together. She'd wanted desperately to see that delight on Jared's face again. She just wished she could've revived it, that she hadn't had to send him away from home for it to happen, and that she didn't worry he would regress when he left the farm and Harte left.

She looked to her mom, and the understanding in her eyes grabbed Maggie by the throat. More tears threatened. She fled to the bench she'd visited so often, detouring to the tool shed long enough to grab a hammer.

Betty, Mike's mom who lived in a house on the opposite side of the farm, met her outside the shed, silently followed with a raised brow, to the bench Mike had built. The silence on the sunny day reminded her of being caught in the eye of hurricane. The moment of peace which came between the bursts of disaster.

With the latest developments, the last thing Maggie needed was to be alone with Mike's mom. She adored Betty as much as her own mother, but keeping secrets from her was impossible and she wasn't ready to talk.

"You're pushing yourself too hard, Maggie."

"I'm fine." She swiped at her lingering tears. "Jared's smiling again."

"It's the puppies." Betty wrapped her arm around her waist. "It's great to see him moving past his grief."

"It is. I should have let him come earlier." Defeated, she

dropped the hammer and sank onto the bench.

"He wouldn't have been happy until he was ready." Betty lifted Maggie's face and brushed a loose hair from her face. "It had nothing to do with being here."

"I'm so confused." Her son was returning to the rambunctious boy he used to be. She shouldn't be sad.

"I'm guessing Detective Harte is the biggest cause of that."

Maggie hesitated, then nodded, hoping she didn't hurt Betty if she voiced her opinion. She fiddled with the end of her braid and faced the truth. Harte had moved into her heart more than she'd wanted. Knowing he wouldn't want to be there hurt more than any loss.

"Why does caring for him scare you? You've always been sure of what you wanted."

"He's confusing. Kind and gentle one minute, rude and bossy the next. He's nothing like Mike."

"Perhaps those differences are part of his appeal." Betty squeezed her hand and smiled. "Part of why you fell in love with him."

"I didn't say…" Maggie leapt off the bench and paced. She cared about Harte, but love… "No." She batted her hair over her shoulder. "It's too soon."

Betty raised her hands in silent surrender. "I watched you and Mike grow up together. You were best friends who slid into marriage easily. You were safe with Mike, but he's been gone a year. You're a different woman."

She gaped at her mother-in-law who was encouraging her to be with Harte. "Harte's an arrogant jerk. I haven't known him near long enough to love him."

"He is also kind and generous by your own admission." Betty braced her elbows on her knees and smiled serenely. "You were the perfect woman for my son, but you deserve a stronger man."

"Mike was…"

"Special. And he never gave you the passion your spirit

begged for. You loved him, but the mention of his name never made you flush the way the mention of Harte's does."

She could neither agree nor disagree. The whole conversation was just too weird. "He's keeping secrets." She couldn't trust a man who didn't trust her.

"It's what cops do. As a homicide cop, you probably don't want him to tell you everything." Betty walked over and hugged her tight. "Talk to him. Tell him what you want. You may be surprised."

Maggie watched her mother-in-law walk away. If only things could be as simple as telling Harte what she wanted. He retreated instantly at the quickest glimpse of intimacy. Besides she had to *know* what she wanted before communicating it became possible. And then there were the dangers he faced daily. Involvement with someone she could so easily lose... No. Not happening beyond the length of his case.

"There you are." Harte's sexy voice startled her from the personal thoughts and shoved her mind back to the real reason for their visit.

"Hey." He approached her with Emma cradled in his arms. How was it a man carrying a baby was such a turn on?

"Are you okay? You seemed sad in there."

"I'm fine." She ran a finger down Emma's cheek. She itched to hold her baby, but he looked happier than she'd ever seen him. Stress drifted away, leaving lightness in her spirit. His happiness filled her with peace unlike years of agreeing with Mike had. *Was* this love? "Who had Emma?"

"Phil. I didn't realize Mike's parents had a house here as well."

"Phil and my dad have always been friends. They invented some gadget the government bought. They made a good deal." She smiled when Emma reached for her. "Mom and Betty shared their dreams for this place."

Sorrow darkened his cobalt eyes as he passed Emma over. Tucking her daughter to her chest, she narrowed her eyes and studied Harte. Suddenly, it occurred to her why he seemed so scarred at times. "You were married."

"Yeah." He didn't look away like she'd expected him to.

"You wanted children?"

He dropped to the bench. Bracing his elbows on his knees so his hands hung down, his shoulders drooped. "Almost had one."

Seated beside him, curious at his candor she edged closer. "What happened?"

"Her name was Samantha. She was Craig's sister." His voice sounded gruff. "We were married for nine months when she told me she was three months pregnant."

He drew in a breath so long and deep his entire body shuddered. "I was working a case that was getting dicey. She refused to go visit her parents out of town."

Maggie's gut clenched. She knew where this was heading.

"I was late picking her up from work one night." His voice broke. "The man we were after got to her."

Sadness and helplessness and devastation floated in the blue sea of his eyes. The grief crowded in her mind with memories of her own. No wonder he fought for distance. She reminded him of what he'd lost. "Did you catch him?"

"I heard the gunshots as I walked into her office." He stared straight ahead. His body shook and his hands fisted as he relived the experience. "I rushed in, weapon drawn. He turned the gun on me. She was lying at his feet."

"You killed him."

"Shot him in the heart."

His stark admission didn't bother her, but she suspected it bothered him. Not so much from his tone or body language as from gaining a better insight into the non-cop side of him. She wanted the closure he'd gotten, to look into the eyes of her husband's killer.

He shrugged and scrubbed a hand over his eyes. "Sam used to say I was her safe haven. I wasn't safe enough."

Maggie squeezed Emma closer. How could she not remind him of his loss? He'd suffered the loss of a child, and the agony of never knowing if the child he would have worshiped would have had his eyes. He saw his need to protect her as a duty, and her insistence to maintain some day-to-day normalcy took him back to his wife. "Harte."

She touched his hand. A shiver coursed through his body. He gripped her hand tightly and closed his eyes. "Being with you... Mags, you rip me up inside. You make me remember everything I've lost."

Tears pooled in his eyes as his big hand moved to cup Emma's head. His thumb rubbed back and forth. "The first time I saw Emma, I had a flash of what it might have been like to hold my own child. I resented you even while I knew how you must have suffered."

"We survived." She cupped her hand over his on Emma and hoped he knew she included him.

"Yeah, and we're going to survive this." He grabbed the hammer she'd brought out effectively severing the moment. "Now, where are the scrolls?"

Her focus fuzzed into grainy thoughts as she shifted away from emotional territory to crime fighting. "We're sitting on them."

"Excuse me?"

"Mike built this bench for us. No problems existed here, only peace. There's never been a safer place than this farm." She stood. When Harte did the same she used her foot to knock the bench over so the legs faced up. "Pop the legs off and I bet you'll find the scrolls."

He tapped each leg with the hammer, listening for sounds of one being hollow. With a nod, he dropped the hammer, stepped into the center of the bench, standing on the base of the seat and aimed well-placed, powerful kicks at two of the legs. They snapped off.

A scroll popped out of the top of each leg. They'd been wrapped in cloth and then plastic. She'd sat on the reason for Mike's death many of times over the last year. If she'd known, if he'd trusted her to handle something beyond a meal plan, if he'd just told her what was going on… *Think about that later.*

"Are you sure the other legs are empty?"

"Yeah," Harte said. "They're solid."

"Then let's go find answers."

With BD at her elbow and sleep deprivation from a night of trying to decipher the symbols on the scrolls and Jared's ceiling dogging her steps, Maggie opened the front door to find Craig dressed in shorts and a T-shirt, holding a case of soda and sporting an outrageously infectious grin, as if he'd come over for a cookout or something equally fun.

"Did someone forget to tell me we were having a party?" Shaking her head, she looked between the two men. "As hostess, I require time to properly prepare these things."

"Sorry, Maggie." Craig winked at her. "We like to be spontaneous."

"Yeah." She reached up and patted his cheek un-gently. "Stop. You always bring bad news and it's exhausting."

"We're doing our best." Craig sobered as he stepped inside when she moved back. "BD."

"Craig." BD's eyes shifted deeper into cop mode. His stance adopted an edge of violence as he closed the inches to her side. "Any luck figuring out who Adalia's inside man is?"

"No, but Cap's on board with our plan."

"You already have a plan?" Maggie closed and locked the door shaking her head. "I guess now I know why you were on the phone so long last night."

"Yeah." Craig pulled an envelope from a side pocket in his shorts. "This was left at the front desk at the station. Do you mind if I borrow BD for a bit?"

"I think I might." Irritation that they seemed to be continuing the secret keeping was cut off by the doorbell.

"You expecting anyone?" Harte's oppressive side was ruling him.

She raised a brow at him. "I didn't know I was expecting

Craig."

He went to the door and glanced out the window. "It's Grace."

"Crap. I'll just go put these in the fridge" Craig darted to the kitchen with the sodas.

Maggie looked from his retreating back to Harte standing sentry and then at the door. "My sister, whom I love dearly, is a meddler. She won't back off if she gets wind of what's really going on or any plan you have."

He sighed. "Let her in. We'll handle it."

She opened the door with what she hoped was a convincing smile. "Hey, Grace."

"Don't mess with me." Grace breezed past, looking around the house. "I want to know what is going on around here. Where's Craig? Craig!" Grace bellowed without waiting for responses. "Get your ass out here!"

Maggie blinked. She wasn't saying anything until she knew what Grace knew. And how she'd found out, though she had a strong suspicion judging by the angry blush on her sister's cheeks.

"Good morning, Maggie, how are you?" She mocked Grace, hoping to buy some time. "Oh, I'm great, Grace. Thanks for asking. What brings you over?"

"You aren't funny." Grace braced her legs apart and tapped her fingers on her crossed arms. "Something is going on around here, and I'm going to find out what. Or I'm calling Dad."

Harte closed the door and jerked his head toward the kitchen. Maggie rolled her eyes and, still in the dark as to BD's plans, led the way to where Craig waited. Whatever he'd done, he was going to suffer one way or another.

Grace shoved past her when she saw Craig by the island. "You son-of-a..."

"Grace!" Maggie protested as she stumbled. BD steadied her with a solid and lingering save when she would have slammed into the wall.

Grace ignored the sisterly assault, marched up to Craig standing by the counter and slapped him across the face. "You used me."

"Get out of firing range." BD murmured as he took Maggie's hand and pulled her to the other side of the island. As protection against Grace's temper was concerned, the island wasn't great, but it did provide shelter to duck if she started throwing things.

"Grace," Craig smiled, oozing charm. "I thought you were sleeping. What are you doing here?"

"Following you. You deceitful, dick-for-brains, piece of scum!"

Maggie choked back a laugh. Her eyes darted between her sister and Craig. Harte calmly watched the exchange, as if he wasn't remotely surprised. "They're...dating? Did you know about this?"

"You used me!"

"No." He covered his lips with a finger, shushing her. Not that they seemed to be disturbing Grace and her tirade.

"You have a conversation with *him* during a date." Grace's finger pointed at Harte as if everyone in the room didn't know who she meant with her disgusted *him*. "Then, after we've...when I ask what's going on, you lie to me."

"Now, Gracie."

Maggie winced. No one, absolutely no one ever called Grace "Gracie". Only one person had been given that right and it had ended violently.

"Don't. You. *Ever.* Call. Me. That." Each word was delivered low and threatening with utter calm and drove the force of the punch she planted in Craig's gut. To his credit, he sucked it up and didn't wince. Much.

Craig held his hands up as if to ward her off. "Calm down."

"Calm down. You *dare* to tell *me* to calm down?" Grace's voice began to rise again. She slid her gaze, her eyes bulging with irrational wrath, across the island. She paused at the knife block.

Maggie moved the knives to the counter behind her and smiled sweetly. She'd rather not be cleaning blood off her floor.

Craig tried on a smile of his own and circled around Grace, keeping out of the reach of her arms.

"He needs to watch out for her legs," Maggie muttered out the side of her mouth. "She's the one who taught me to kick."

"Oh, this is gonna be good." BD chuckled and wrapped a companionable arm around her shoulders, pulling her close. Her belly rumbled with pleasure. Maybe from the easy touch. Maybe from the suggested connection.

"I did not lie. Or use you." Craig's smooth voice would have calmed anyone else, but Grace wasn't going to cool off anytime soon.

"Bull!" She pointed over at Maggie and Harte again. "You canceled on spending the day with me to come over here. You're both armed and checking into Mike."

Craig had spent the night with Grace? *Whoa.* She hadn't allowed a man in her home since…well, since Alex Kord, the violent ending.

"How would you know I checked into Mike?"

"Wrong move, cutie," Maggie mumbled. Questioning Grace when she was mad could be lethal.

Grace spun through the air, leading with a foot aimed at Craig's head.

Maggie winced.

Craig ducked.

Harte laughed.

Landing back on both feet, tapping her fingers on her hips, Grace stared at Craig—not remotely put off by his size advantage or the fact she'd missed her target. The desire to take another kick ramped up in her blazing stare. "I read your emails while you were snoring in my bed."

BD roared with laughter. Maggie choked back her own laugh. They'd have to tell Grace everything. It was the only way to keep Craig's body parts where they belonged, and she liked him too much to see him maimed. She especially liked that he'd clearly broached some of Grace's defenses.

Grace spun toward her and Harte. "You think this is funny? Maggie, do you know they've run a major background check on Mike? Harte's been searching your house when you're gone or asleep."

She turned to face BD. He sobered instantly.

Grace stood on the other side of the island, chest heaving, smug pleasure spreading her lips. Craig looked on, probably eager to see someone else besides him get their ass chewed out.

"You could have told me that part." He'd lied to her about suspecting her husband. She should feel angry or betrayed. She felt...protected.

"What?" Grace gasped.

Harte slid his hand down her arm and linked his fingers with her. "I would have if I learned something that would change things."

Definitely protected. The necessity hurt, but knowing he'd wanted to watch out for her eased the sting. It was nice to rank so high for someone. "You still could have told me."

"What is going on around here?" Grace shrieked her question. "I feel like I'm in a crazy sitcom."

"We're going to get her, Mags." BD moved his hands to her hips and held her gaze.

"I trust you." *I love you. Whoa! Back up, Maggie.* Hadn't expected that. She sure didn't know what to do with it at the moment.

"Hello!" Grace smacked her hands on the counter top to get their attention. "Remember me?"

"Oh, all right." Maggie snapped as she turned to her sister. "You get the Cliff Notes version. You'll not pepper me with questions or badger me with your constant presence."

"You're giving me orders?"

"It's a new concept, but yeah." Maggie grinned. Tingles traipsed along her arms and neck and spine. Strength. If the moment weren't so charged she'd close her eyes and relish the development. "And you're going to follow them."

Grace tapped her meticulously manicured nails against the tile counter. "Fine. Spill it."

Craig moved closer to Grace, as if he needed to protect her. She shifted fractionally closer. They'd be good together, if he could get her to not run, but that was for another day. In a two-minute summary, Maggie told Grace everything she knew.

"What?" Grace lurched toward the counter. Craig laid a hand on her arm. She smacked him away, but when she looked back it was with concern filling her gaze. "You didn't think I needed to know this?"

"What were you going to do, Grace? Harte's here." Maggie glanced at him, inches away. "Hovering constantly with a loaded gun. Craig's a phone call away. They're doing everything they can to catch Adalia and protect me."

"This is why the kids are at the farm. You tell Dad and Phil?"

"Yes."

"We don't expect Adalia to stray far from Maggie," Craig said. "The kids are safe."

"I mean it." Grace turned on him. "Back off. You should have told me."

"Grace," BD rested his elbows on the counter and leaned forward. "He couldn't tell you any more than I was supposed to tell Maggie."

"But you did tell her."

"Different circumstances." He turned his head toward Maggie. "And it'll be over. Soon."

Maggie sucked in a pained and iced breath that stabbed deep in her heart. More than the case would be over. He would leave, taking any chance of a *them* with him.

Maggie closed the door behind Grace and locked it before turning to face BD. "What's in the envelope?"

"Let's find out." Holding his hand toward the kitchen, he waited for her to precede him to where Craig had chosen to stay as a way of avoiding more of Grace's wrath. His only surprise at the Craig and Grace coupling was how polar opposite she was from the reserved kindergarten teacher types he normally went for. The Malones bred strong women.

How strong?

They had to know what was in the envelope, but BD's instinct to shield Maggie warred with the fact she'd figure it out anyway. She was getting under his skin. The more time he spent around her, the more he wanted to be with her. She especially disturbed him when she paced the house in the middle of the night.

Checking blinds and locks he'd already checked or sitting in the chairs in each kid's room—sad and alone in the silence until he drew her into watching one of her many action DVDs.

Every minute in her company made resistance increasingly difficult.

Back in the kitchen, standing at the island, with Maggie at his side and Craig on the other side of the counter, BD pulled the envelope closer. "You sure about this, Mags?"

"We can do it without you," Craig added.

"No."

"Adalia doesn't play fair." BD stopped himself from giving her the warning of how Adalia tortured her victims mentally, emotionally and physically. Maggie had experienced a little of the first two. She would never know the last.

"Message received."

As vitally as he knew hoping she wouldn't argue was pointless.

Craig leaned forward and covered her hand with his. "Bear that in mind the next time you give BD hell."

"Surely he hasn't been whining. I think I've gone along pretty well."

"Mostly. A blind man can see how you enjoy tormenting him." Craig winked at her. "I'm not blind."

"If you two don't mind." BD tapped the envelope.

Maggie pulled latex gloves out of a box in a drawer for each of them. After putting them on, BD withdrew a piece of blood red cloth. Gripping the scratchy linen, he pulled back the folds.

3 - TICK TOCK

The typed words covered a plain white sheet of paper. Flipping the paper over, the image of peaceful suburban life with a wife on the outskirts of the fun stared up at him. The photo was of Mike and Jared playing ball on the front lawn. Maggie stood off to the side, hands clasped in front of her, shadows lingered in her eyes, and her shoulders were slightly slouched.

Those shoulders still carried a heavy load, heavier now than then, but she no longer slouched or accepted defeat. As if proving the point, she stepped closer and turned the photo, a likely souvenir from one of Adalia's visits to her home, toward her with the tip of her nail.

"I've never seen this picture, but I remember this day. It was the day before Mike's death."

"This wasn't yours?"

Her eyes filled with determined suspicion. "No."

"She was watching Mike." *No surprise there.*

Craig stepped around the counter to stand on Maggie's other side. "And knew his time was running out."

"Sorry, Mags."

She shook her head and waved BD on to the next page.

2 - REACT FASTER

Slipping the second sheet of white paper aside, BD's knees and legs dissolved. He grabbed the edge of the counter and closed his eyes. Darkness whirled with memories, loss and hate. The sketch Samantha had drawn mocked him. It was one of the few things he'd kept from that life, but he hadn't been able to stomach looking at the eerily lifelike rendering of a blue-eyed infant.

Maggie looked between them with confusion stamped on her features. "I don't get it."

"It's a long story for later," Craig said.

Much later. "Adalia took this the day I moved in." It was her way of reminding them Maggie wasn't the only target. "Bitch gets points for knowing where to strike."

And she'd just dealt her losing hand. BD slid the paper to the side.

1 – SOON

Uncovering the last picture, seeing him and Maggie sitting close together on the picnic table, anger broiled through his veins. It had been snapped from high in one of the neighboring trees as they'd talked about Mike. The moment he'd opened up enough to trust Maggie while breaking her heart again was forever caught on film.

Craig's eyes flashed to his and he knew his friend had seen the truth. With it staring him in the face, impossible to ignore, he recognized for the first time what he'd been working so hard to deny. He cared deeply for Maggie and every quirky, obsessive-compulsive part of her.

"She's trying to push us with this," Craig kept the conversation on business while his store promised a long talk later. "This was delivered to the station before I went in to update Cap on our plan."

"She'll know very soon, if she doesn't already, we have the scrolls." A best friend capable of reading your thoughts could be a pain in the ass. He also made the best wingman a guy could ask for by keeping the really big secrets. "Mags. Are you all right?"

She met his eyes boldly. Nope. Pure, unadulterated rage fired in her generally peaceful and sometimes sad gaze. "I will be."

"I'll call and update Cap." Craig pulled his phone from his pocket and headed to the other room.

BD took Maggie's hand and led her to the table. Sitting beside her, the damning need to stop the woman responsible for threatening her clenched his gut. "No one would blame you for being scared."

"Are you? Scared?"

"I'd be dead if this stuff didn't scare me."

She pinched the bridge of her nose, something he always did. "I don't understand."

"We're afraid every time we go into a potentially dangerous situation. Instead of letting it rule us, we use it to focus on the job." Failure meant death, and as much as he'd dreaded life at times death had never really been an option.

"How? What do you do to force yourself beyond the fear?"

Wanting, needing, the reassurance of her nearness, hoping to reassure her in return, he bracketed her knees between his own and rubbed his hands over her thighs. "If we fail, people lose their lives. It's a harsh reality, but by keeping it in mind, by remembering to be smarter than whoever we're after, we have the advantage. No one else will die at Adalia's hands."

She linked her fingers with his over her legs, connecting them with a quiet intimacy. "Her mind games bug me. How do I stop that?"

He wasn't sure when they'd stopped fighting their attraction, but he would enjoy the moments. "You've already done it. You refuse to let her run you off. That's courage."

He raised her hand, kissing her knuckles as it was the only way he could show her how much he cared. "I'll keep you safe, Mags."

She smiled and her entire face softened like it did in rare instances of relaxed happiness she slowed herself. "Tell me what we do to end this. I want my life back."

Chapter Eleven

Maggie had been reading Mike's translations over and over for hours when the phone rang. Intent on the symbol to letter code sheet Mike hadn't finished, she grabbed it without checking caller ID. "Hello."

"You and Detective Harte make a lovely couple." She'd never spoken to Adalia Wood, but the cultivated charm was the same she'd heard in the courtroom. The charm did nothing to hide her evilness. "Such passion."

A cold shiver coursed down Maggie's spine as she spun around. The window blinds were closed, as were all the blinds in the house. "Excuse me?"

Harte dropped the notes he'd been re-reading into the armchair, crossed the room in two strides and towered over her, dominating her space and the room. "Adalia," he mouthed silently.

Maggie nodded and focused on the call. Harte pulled his cell phone from his pocket and punched in a few numbers.

"Have you gotten my notes?"

"They're vague." Leaning against the desk, she wondered at her absence of thoughts. Shouldn't her mind be racing with them? "Why don't you tell me why you want these papers?"

"I like that you don't play games. That you don't pretend to not have them."

Harte circled his hand in front of her, prompting her to keep Adalia talking. All the while he spoke into his phone so quietly she wondered how whoever he spoke to heard him, because even inches away she couldn't.

"It would only delay the inevitable." The final confrontation with Adalia had been delayed enough. She wasn't ready to see BD, but was more than ready for life to normalize.

"You're right," Adalia agreed amiably, "but it won't save

your life."

Icy chills scraped along Maggie's skin. Fear grabbed her by the throat. She leaned forward, struggling to breathe beyond the pain pricks stabbing at her intestines. Buzzing in her ears almost drowned out her thoughts.

The buzzing was Adalia's voice. "You're a beautiful woman with cute kids, Maggie. You have a lot of self-control. More than your slut sister."

Harte's hand landed on her back. Strong. She glanced into his eyes. Calm. Straightening, she shot her fears the middle finger. "You like watching me, Adalia? Would you prefer it if I opened the blinds and gave you more of a show?"

"I wonder what it takes to send you over the edge." The charm gave away to tightly suppressed rage and Maggie pictured Adalia's knuckles whitening on the phone.

"You can find out when you come get the papers."

"The clock's ticking."

"Care to tell me how long I have?" She was losing any control she'd had over the call with Adalia's ramping anger.

"I didn't plan on killing Mike. I liked him." She ignored Maggie's question. "I can't say the same about you and Harte."

"We both know you'd have killed him once you had the papers." Dread cooled Maggie's blood. Harte lightly thumped her chin, pulling her attention back to Adalia. If she had something the woman wanted, then she was relatively safe. At least until she got it. "Is there a point to this conversation other than your weak attempt to get inside my head?"

"You will fear me."

Maggie's bravado held out long enough for her to ease a casual shrug into her tone, needling Adalia. "Listen, I have a lot to do. Why don't you come over? We'll end this now."

"Get rid of your bodyguard."

"Harte scares you?"

"I don't like prison."

"And here I thought you'd be more than just a talking ego." Maggie laughed. "Besides, he can't put you behind bars if you kill him."

Maggie's guts knotted with sickness at the idea of BD being killed.

"You'll beg me for mercy before you die, Maggie." Adalia's ego invaded her growl of frustration. "Don't try any tricks."

The phone went silent.

BD held in the curse. No trace. Adalia had likely used a burner phone and the signal bounced between towers. She'd been on the move while he was feeling more like a rat cage in a glass-encased maze with Adalia tapping the lid to create confusion.

Suppressing useless aggravation, he knelt before Maggie. He ached to pull her close and comfort her, but instead made her recount the conversation.

"It's okay, Mags." He cupped her face and held her gaze. "She's trying to freak you out before she makes her move."

"I think it's working."

"No. You can do this." Though if they'd had time to bring in an undercover cop to act as decoy he would have done it. "She won't make a move as long as I'm here."

"You can't be here twenty-four seven."

He sank back onto his heels. The pressure to save her, to avoid involvement, built until he couldn't ignore the desire anymore. "How can I help you feel better? What can I do to take your mind off everything for a little bit?"

She could ask for anything, and he'd walk barefoot through running lava to give it to her.

"Kiss me again."

He hadn't expected that.

An inch away, so close he smelled the fragrant scent she always wore, the image of her blood had him pulling back. He could give her anything but that. Moving to the next level with her blurred the lines of why he was here. Protect her. Catch a killer. Nothing more. "Mags."

She slid a fingertip over his mouth, pleading with her eyes. "Please."

Tracing a thumb over her bottom lip, plump from her chewing teeth, he yearned. To feel her. To give her pleasure. To know that in the midst of her pain and loss *he* was able to give her something special.

Don't do it.

A molten core of passion rested untapped just below the surface of her skin. Rapture drifted through him at the thought of being the one to awaken her.

"Be sure, Mags." *This is a mistake!* "If I kiss you, it isn't going to stop there."

"I know." Her tongue darted out and brushed the tip of his thumb. "I want you."

Heat and arousal shot south. Logic scattered. He stood and pulled her to her feet before sliding her up his body. Holding her hips, he pulled her close so she was pressed tight to him. "Wrap your legs around me. We're going for a ride."

She locked her ankles behind his waist. Smiling, she rubbed against his erection. Warm moisture penetrated her clothes and seeped into him.

Determined not to drop her, or fall to the floor because of weak knees, he headed for his room.

She tightened her legs, digging the gun he'd tucked at his waist into his spine. The pain almost centered him in reality. But holding her in his arms, knowing this was a moment's escape from threats and danger, promised pure pleasure. He intended for them both to enjoy.

This wasn't a permanent relationship, but neither was she a hit-and-run screw. After he left—and he would leave because a happily-ever-after with a ready-made family wasn't in his future—she would not remember him as selfish in bed.

Carrying her down the hall, her soft curves fitting against him naturally, her fingers tangled in his hair and soft brushes of her fingertips against his neck shot sparks of fire through his veins.

His gaze moved over her face. The tip of her tongue darted across her lips. Her mouth parted again in anticipation.

Primitive need snaked through him. His heart rate rocketed. He wanted to kiss her. Taste her.

"Screw it." Pinning her to the wall, rocking his hips, and rubbing against the hot moisture wetting her jeans, he claimed her mouth.

Their tongues dueled. Muscle sliding against muscle. She moaned and arched against him. His knees buckled and slammed into the wall. No woman had ever launched him as far into full arousal as Maggie had with a whispered request for a kiss.

"Mmm." Tilting her head, she nibbled along his neck. "Burke."

Angling his head to the side, he closed his eyes and thrilled at her touch, at the sound of his name rolling off her tongue when she'd only called him Harte before. "Mags. Bed."

"Okay." Her warm breath rushed across his ear. She kept nibbling on him like he was some kind of feast.

Fisting his hand in her shirt, he mustered up the strength to move to his room. At the end of his bed, he resisted the urge to toss her down and devour her like a starved animal. "Unlink your ankles."

When he slid her to the floor, she kept her right leg hooked at his hip. Her left hand slid around his waist and pulled him closer. Pressing against his raging erection, she looked into his eyes and sent him a feline grin.

"Damn, you're gorgeous." The words scraped his throat unrecognizable as his voice. Too late to turn back, he knew he was going to burn for this pleasure.

Cupping her ass, BD pulled her tighter against him, lifting her so he could claim her mouth. With a purring sigh, she opened to him, welcoming him with her warmth. He explored the sweetness of her mouth. Running the tip of his tongue over her lips, he pushed his way through the slight opening.

She arched into him. Her pebbled nipples brushed his chest, singeing him. If they were naked he'd be well on the way to heaven, but since they weren't he had that much longer to discover the hidden treasures of her body.

Fisting his hand in her braid, he tipped her head back for fuller access to her mouth. Showing her a hint of how thoroughly he planned to enjoy her, he thrust his tongue in and out of her mouth.

She thrust her hips forward in a mirrored answer. Her moist heat teased him through their pants and made him glad he still wore his pajama bottoms. Pulling back, he traced her lips with a finger and held her gaze.

Uncertainty flashed for a second, but it was enough to cool him off. "Be very sure, Mags. If you want to stop, now's the time to say so."

Without blinking, she traced his lips as he'd done hers. "I want this."

This. Not him. He should be grateful for the distance her words insinuated. Instead, they stabbed at him and cooled his ardor enough for clarity. He sat her gently away, so they were close, but not touching. She wasn't a casual sex kind of woman, and he was going to prove it to her. She would want *him* before they were finished.

"I'm going to taste every inch of you." He placed a finger by her eye. "Starting here."

Her eyes flared with aroused awareness. Using only the tip of his tongue to touch her, he caressed her. She gasped.

"I look forward to it."

Moving back, he smiled as he pointed to her nose. "This arouses me when you tip it up in defiance. And your eyes when they darken with arousal, like now."

"Harte."

"Relax, Mags." Quirking a brow, he grinned. She'd use his given name again too. "I finally have you willing. I am *not* rushing this."

"But…" The plea in her eyes darkened and mixed with

confusion. "I thought…"

The sex she'd offered was turning into a seduction. He would spend all day seducing her if need be. Rather than move in for the next taste, he tilted his head. "What, Mags? Say it."

"I thought it would be quick. Simple."

"Is that what you're used to? What you prefer?" Was it what she'd always known? A quickie with no seduction? No passion? Was that why she responded with such abandon? Did she read the romance novels on her shelves for escape, or because she saw herself as the women on the page?

"I…" She hesitated. "I like sex. It's just always been…"

"A fulfillment of basic needs?" Okay, maybe a little harsh.

"Yes."

"Not this time." Her sadness had a disturbing ache settling in his chest, as if he really cared. Rather, as if he wanted to care and it was too much to handle at the moment. He would give her passion. Nothing more. "I need one thing from you before we go any further."

"W-what?" Her voice trembled, but she didn't blink or look away.

"Trust me not to let you down." Unable to not touch her a moment longer, he dredged up more of his rarely tapped tenderness and laid his palm on her cheek. "And tell me if you want me to do something different, or if you want more of something."

Embarrassment flushed her cheeks. She didn't have to tell him what she'd been missing all these years. Her uncertainty reminded him of his high school girlfriend the night she'd given him her virginity. And in many ways he suspected he would be Maggie's first. He needed to make it count.

"Do you trust me, Mags?" He ignored the little voice insisting he was asking for more than her body.

"Yes."

Giving himself the space he needed to take things slowly for her, he held her gaze as he dropped his hand and backed to the small desk to lay his gun down. He stood, waiting for her to bolt and prove she didn't trust him.

The pulse in her neck hammered. Her eyes trailing over him and filling with renewed passion thrilled him. Cocking a brow, he pulled the drawstring of his pants while kicking his shoes to the side.

She swallowed, but she stayed.

Her nipples tightened beneath her shirt. Holding her gaze, praying she didn't run, he pushed his pants to the floor before straightening to let her look her fill.

He wanted this memory to be as perfect for himself as he did for her.

The flush covering her cheeks deepened and spread down her neck until it disappeared beneath the collar of her shirt. Her breasts had swollen. Her nipples hardened more and pressed against her bra. Her tongue teased her bottom lip as she devoured every naked inch of him.

Her chest rose and fell rapidly as she stared at his erection and then a wicked grin spread across her mouth. He didn't have to wonder if she liked it or not.

"You're…" She fisted her hands at her sides and slid her eyes back up until they met his. "Wow."

"Thanks." Staying back any longer was impossible.

He closed the distance between them and reached out to rub his thumb over a pebbled nipple. As impossible as it seemed, it hardened more. Running his hands down her sides, he pulled the waist of her tidily tucked in T-shirt from her jeans. Sliding the shirt up her torso, he slid his fingertips over the newly exposed skin.

Her pupils flared and dilated. Her skin rippled beneath his touch. His own body burned to move things along faster, but he had to give her this moment. He had to prove she hadn't made a mistake by giving him her trust. "Raise your arms, Mags."

She did as he asked. He pulled her shirt to her wrists, but rather than removing it, he lowered her arms in front of her and positioned her hands at her sides, spread as far as possible with her shirt acting as handcuffs. Escape would be easy, but the idea of her being bound and at his will, was an easy way to test trust.

"You're like porcelain." Teasing himself as much as her, he leaned close to her ear. "I can't wait to see if you look like this all over."

"Burke." She turned her head and brushed a kiss beneath his ear. More flames shot through his body, arousing him more.

Burke, not Harte. She was right where he wanted her. "Do you like this?"

"Yes." Her normally sultry voice thickened with a plea.

She could beg, but he still wasn't rushing. "Then you'll love what comes next."

Since he was so close to her ear, he traced the outer edge with his tongue while rolling her nipple with his thumb. She moaned and angled toward him.

He backed away.

"Turn around, Mags."

Her eyes flashed to his as if she was going to argue. He raised a brow and waited. He hadn't seduced a woman in…well, ever.

When she turned, he dropped his head back and blew out a breath. This was going to kill him.

He slid his palms up her back and down again to the end of her braid near her waist. Pulling the hair band out and tossing it to the floor, he worked her braid free until he could fan her hair out so it covered her bare back.

Stepping close, his chest rubbing hers, he brushed her hair aside and whispered into her ear. "I love your hair."

Her shudder echoed through his body. Slipping his fingers back to the hook of her bra, he twisted the material and popped it loose. He rested his hands on her shoulders and pushed the straps of her bra off her shoulders and down her arms, until they stopped at her shirt.

Turning her back to face him, the nipples he'd watched harden stood at attention begging for his touch. Her breasts swayed with her uneven breaths. He nearly swallowed his own tongue imagining how she would taste.

He twitched with eagerness to feel more of her, and to feel her touch him. Taking a small hunk of hair in each hand, he slid the ends of her hair over her nipples. The tiny bumps circling the tip popped out.

She gasped. Her breasts swelled. Her eyes slid shut. Her head fell back.

"Do you like that? Or do you want something different?"

"Yes."

"Yes, you like it? Or yes, you want something different?" Without waiting for her response, he slid his tongue around one hardened pink nipple.

She jerked toward him, encouraging.

"You like that?"

Taking her moan as a positive answer, he slid his tongue across her breasts to her other nipple. She thrust toward him. As much as he wanted to hover, he wanted to discover her other delights more.

He moved back to the center of her chest and covered her torso with nibbling kisses. He never stopped brushing her hair over her breasts. "Tell me, Mags. What's that feel like?"

"W-what?"

"Your hair on your breasts. How's it feel?"

She rolled her hips. A soft moan escaped her lips. "Soft. It tickles."

"And?"

"Erotic. Decadent." She jerked her hands, but didn't pull them free of the shirt. "As if your mouth is hovering over me blowing warm air."

"Like this?" Lowering to his knees, he laved at her belly button and blew a warm breath over the moisture.

She shivered. "Yes."

"And where else would you like me to touch you, kiss you, blow on you?" Slipping his fingers in the edge of her pants at her sides, he edged toward the button, all the while pressing kisses to the quivering mass of muscles in her abdomen.

"Everywhere." She freed herself from the makeshift cuffs and fisted her hands in his hair. She would give him everything he wanted and more. She would come unglued. He would take her to ecstasy.

He released the button of her jeans and lowered the zipper. She'd expected a mad dash to the finish line. So had he. This was so much better.

Covering her with more nibbling kisses, he eased her pants down her legs. He'd missed her stepping out of her shoes, but wasn't complaining. She braced herself on him, her right hand clutching his shoulder with her little finger tracing the edge of a scar he'd thought to be numb, and stepped free of the pants.

Fuck. She stood before him in nothing but the lace thong he'd unpinned the note from. Gliding his tongue along the edge, he exhaled slowly. "Here?"

"Yes!" Her hips jerked toward his mouth.

He almost gave in to the temptation to taste her while kneeling between her legs. To take her all the way over with his mouth, but he needed to make it last.

"So soft. You feel like silk." He slid his fingers over her bare skin as he stood. Meeting her burning gaze, he smiled. "I'm going to ease you into a quivering mass of arousal until you unravel and cry out my name begging for release."

"Harte." It was a moan, but not the name he wanted.

"Not good enough, Mags." He gestured to the bed behind her. She was aroused enough to do anything he pushed her into, but it would mean more if she made the choice. "Get on the bed. Get comfortable."

With his patience straining on a short leash, he moved to the side table for the condoms. She crawled onto the bed, propped herself against the headboard with her arms crossed over her breasts and her ankles crossed.

Holding a condom against his leg, he held her wary stare. "Last chance to run, Mags."

Even as he said it, he hoped like hell she stayed.

Looking at the condom in Harte's hand, Maggie knew why she hadn't removed them before he moved in. She'd wanted to end up here, in his bed, with him standing before her aroused and ready. She hadn't imagined he would be a patient lover, but regardless of what happened when he climbed onto the bed with her, he'd already given her more than Mike, her only lover, ever had.

Chewing on her lip, she considered his offer. She could bolt. Get up and walk out. But was it worth missing out on the kind of passion she'd always wanted? The kind of heat that lit fires in her soul and spread through her veins? She wanted a passion strong enough to live clearly in her mind even after he left.

She'd been comfortable and certain until he'd stepped back. Without his constant attention doubt snuck in, but the flaming desire in his eyes, and the raging erection facing her, drove home how insane she was behaving.

Releasing her lip, she raised her chin, uncrossed her arms and ankles, and spread her legs. "I'm not going anywhere, Harte."

"Good." He tossed the condom by her hip and moved to the end of the bed, kneeling between her spread knees. "Do you remember what I told you?"

She nodded, remembering vividly the huskiness in his voice as he promised to ease her into a quivering mass of arousal until she cried out his name before begging for release. Forgotten muscles deep in her womb clenched and quivered at the idea. How far did he intend to take her?

As if she'd spoken aloud, he leaned forward and gave her a long lingering kiss. The skin on skin contact she ached for didn't come. The teasing brush of his fingers remained absent. Instead, with agonizing control, his tongue explored her mouth in all the ways she imagined him touching the rest of her.

She gripped his broad shoulders and traced the contours of his biceps. However much time he spent working out was well worth it. She'd never touched a sexier man. Gliding her fingers up to explore his back, she felt a pucker of skin high on his shoulder.

"What happened?" While she traced what was surely a war wound he'd gotten on the job, he broke off the kiss and met her gaze.

"A stray bullet during a robbery."

His matter-of-fact tone, as if scars from flying bullets didn't matter, reiterated the reason she couldn't have more than a passing affair with him. As long as he was willing, they could have sex, but nothing more. She could not, *would* not, risk her heart again.

Not that he seemed to mind.

Beginning a sensual assault on her neck, he didn't give her the chance to ask any more questions. Her head settled deeper into his pillows. Her muscles quivered, relaxed, and quivered again each time he moved his mouth.

Avoiding the scar, she slid her hands over his back, moving toward his hips. His arousal pressed against her.

Putting distance between her hands and the goal of his hips, he eased down her body covering her with nibbling kisses. The occasional nip of his teeth followed by a soothing kiss and warm breath took her desire a notch higher. How, when she'd never been so hot, did he continue to raise her temperature and awareness?

"Harte."

His lips curled in a smile against her stomach, but he shook his head and continued his assault on her body and sizzling nerves. What more could he possibly want?

When his slow descent delivered him to the juncture of her thighs, she arched her hips off the bed. Her fingers pressed against the back of his head, begging him to kiss her where Mike had never wanted to. Her pussy shook with anticipation.

A chuckle rumbled from his chest as he lifted his head, easily resisting her attempts.

He pulled her hands from his head and pinned them to the

mattress by her hips. His desire-darkened cobalt eyes seared her with heat. "Tell me what you want, Mags."

"I want…I need…"

"Yes?"

"Please…kiss me…there."

Grinning, he lowered his head and pressed a kiss to the inside of her right knee, making her leg quiver. "There?"

"No."

He pressed a kiss to her left knee and had that leg quivering. "There?"

"N-no."

"I think I know." He lowered his head and pressed a kiss to her thigh, just where it met her hip. "There?"

She shoved her head into the pillow, her hands fisted beneath his. She bucked her hips again.

"Was that not where you wanted it? Maybe you should be more specific."

"No." She moaned when he blew a warm breath over the slick heat waiting for him.

He pressed a kiss to her other thigh.

"Harte."

She was giving him what he wanted. Her body more than quivered beneath his. She could hardly communicate beyond a moan. Still, he only teased. "Please. Taste me. Eat me. I want to feel your mouth on me."

His warm breath rushed across her. She actually *felt* herself swell and throb. Jeez, she was going to erupt without his touch if he kept it up. Then his tongue flicked across her.

She screamed.

"You like that?"

Her hips bucked toward him. "Yes. Please. More."

He slid his tongue up the length of her. Her muscles clenched in orgasm. "Burke, please."

In seconds, her hands were free of his grasp. The condom wrapper was ripped open. His mouth teased her, drove her higher, while he sheathed himself.

"Hurry," she urged.

He slid up her body, pressing against her. Arousal to arousal. Chest to chest. "My name, Mags. Say my name."

She couldn't have resisted for anything. "Burke. Please, Burke. Now!"

He thrust. Filled her. Froze. Her muscles convulsed. Tense.

Not moving, his cobalt eyes imprisoned hers in a kaleidoscope of emotions. Asking him to kiss her and touch her had seemed so basic. Only it wasn't. She'd never been so free with herself or her wishes. Sex for the sake of sex was gone, and it scared the hell out of her.

Choking back tears and blocking the thoughts of what she'd lost to him, her heart spasmed in time with her body. She locked her ankles behind his waist and pulled herself closer.

His erection throbbed and pulsed inside her. The head of his dick rubbing the spot she'd always heard existed but never felt had her muscles convulsing harder and faster.

Until him, she'd never had a real orgasm.

Then he started gliding in and out. The friction of his sweat-slicked skin rubbing against hers, teasing her nerves, and the sensation of him nudging her g-spot over and over, took her higher than she'd already been.

Locking her gaze with his, she watched his pupils flare and drown out the blue. Digging her fingers into his arms, his banded biceps rippling beneath her fingers, she arched up to be closer still, as if she could get inside his skin.

Burying his face in her neck, his chest rubbing hers, the rumble rising up his chest echoed through her. "Let go, Mags."

He nipped her lobe and thrust into her. Her body trembled with the force of her orgasm. He moaned and jerked with his own release and deep inside she wept. With the surrender of her orgasmic virginity, she'd paid an immeasurable price. One she wasn't sure she could afford.

Chapter Twelve

"Not sure why I bother with this." Maggie muttered as she sorted Transformer from G.I. Joes. "It won't stay clean, and the mess won't matter if I'm dead."

She worked through the mess in Jared's room, her thoughts volleying between BD's plan, her kids and the promise that brought her full circle to fear. Adalia's promise to kill.

BD's assurances did little to calm the seismic quakes attacking her nerved. Any time now, Craig would come for BD. They would leave. She would be alone. Bait for the criminal.

They'd made a show in the bugged living room of calling for an AC repairman and opening all the windows while complaining about the heat. Making the house accessible was one thing. Announcing to Adalia they were trapping her when she was looking for ways to trap them was another. Why had she agreed to risk herself?

Weakness. The taunt whispered along her conscience.

Weakness resulting from Burke's every touch and the constant hunger to be brave around him. There was no other explanation for why she'd given in. Why she'd asked him to kiss her. Why she'd asked him to make love to her when there was no shot at more. It was a mistake she wouldn't make again. Neither would she regret the beautiful seduction.

She sank to the floor, sitting butt to heels and staring into the not-far-from-past memory. Casual sex didn't exist inside the richness of what they'd shared. Touch and taste. Sight and sound. She'd felt it all as thick as tears in her throat.

She should have known better. She would have if she'd actually thought. Instead, she'd grabbed the chance for a mental escape, gone off less than half-cocked without regard to the consequences, followed her gut and given her trust to a man she hardly knew. All for a fleeting glimpse of euphoria.

He offered the illusion of safety, reeled her in until she'd gotten lost in him and it had cost more of her heart.

Mike had literally been the boy next door. They'd gone from friends, to dates of convenience, to married. The realities of sex she knew she learned from him, yet the gaps in her knowledge had burst forth in bed with Burke. She'd never been so free with her body, so quick to embrace abandon.

She'd even started calling him BD...Burke.

"Mags." His voice—one she would hear often in dreams—deep with sexual suggestions drew her gaze to the doorway.

H-O-L-Y H-E-L-L. Burke...BD...Harte. Harte—she had to think of him that way for there to be any hope of coping with the coming loss of bliss he'd stimulated—stood with water droplets dripping down his broad, naked chest. He'd only put on jeans and shoes.

There would be no blocking the memory. Now that she *knew* what lurked beneath the surface of the often solemn detective, his nakedness was harder to face.

"It's almost time. What are you doing?"

"Cleaning. I need to stay busy." Not that it was settling her mind.

As though nothing had happened, as though he hadn't shown her pleasures which made fantasies look tame, he walked around like he owned the place. He'd snapped back into himself—fully in cop mode with no hint that she'd been anything more than a release of energy.

"Last chance. We can find another way."

"There is no other way." She stood and kicked a ball of dirty clothes toward Jared's hamper. "If Adalia has to be stalled until you get into position it's going to have to be done by someone who knows Mike, what he learned from those scrolls and where they are."

"You're asking me for too much." BD closed the distance between them and took her loose hair in his hand. "I can't risk you getting hurt if I'm delayed."

His voice cracked on what she knew to be an uncomfortable admission. Her heart cracked a little.

"I trust you." Brushing his cheek with her fingers she sought to reassure him. "This is something I have to do."

He turned to the dresser and picked up a picture of Mike and Jared grinning like loons. Unsteady breaths moved his back up and down. Up and down. "Did I tell you I sat with Mike while he died?"

She sniffed, but wouldn't cry. "Yes."

"I didn't tell you... In those moments he struck me as an upstanding guy whose only concern was the wife and son he'd never see again." BD traced the edge of the frame, speaking reverently about her husband. Maybe a sliver of regret mingled with reverence. "You consumed his last thoughts, Mags. He loved you. He knew the treasure of what he had in this home."

Tears fell down her heated face. "You don't fight fair."

"I need you to know how much you have to fight for." He still didn't look at her. Didn't look away from the picture he continued rubbing. "I lost my family. Don't do something that's going to cost you yours."

"I'm not going to." She went to him and rested her cheek on his bare back. "I know what I have to lose. I wonder if you do."

"Maggie." He rolled his shoulders and stepped away with a distinct you're dismissed vibe.

"Nevermind. I get it." *Fine. If that's how he wants it, fine.* "You played your games. You got your jollies. Time's up."

"You know damn well it wasn't like that. Not for one second."

"Really? Prove it. Give me one reason to believe anything we did meant something to you." She angled her chin. "Because your lackluster tone holds no conviction and every time I let myself get close or reach out, you pull away. Or shove me away."

"You're wrong."

"Then why do you kiss me?"

"I kiss you because... Damn it." His voice finally held passion. Fire. "I kiss you because I like it." His mouth devoured hers in a brief, punishing kiss before he thrust her away. "I gave you orgasms because you asked for them."

"Burke."

"No! You got what you wanted from me and walked away. You're the one who couldn't get out of my bed fast enough. If anyone was a meaningless lay it was me to you."

"That's not true!" How could he be the one hurt? How could he not know what he'd done to her? How could he have been so aware of her every desire and not know how much it had meant to her?

"You know what? It doesn't matter." His attempt at another dismissal fizzled. It did matter if the hurt in his tone was an indicator. "Think what you want."

"I happen to think you're an ass."

"Damn it, Mags." Shaking his hands in front of her in an almost comical, claw-like fashion he growled. "Why do you have to be so stubborn?"

"Why do you have to be so overbearing?"

"I'm trying to protect you!"

"By demanding where I sleep? Or by screwing me blind? Or by trying to browbeat me into doing everything your way, when and where you want?"

"It's not like that! It hasn't been like that!"

"It's exactly like that!" Realizing she was screaming, she froze. Her heart slammed within her ribcage, banging and clanging. She rubbed at the pain and tried to calm herself. She'd never screamed at anyone. Ever.

Losing control simply wasn't an option, and she'd done it multiple times. What was it about Harte took her over the cliff of rational behavior?

Stare-to-stare, toe-to-toe, they stood. Combative. Breathing deep. Not blinking. Like they were waiting to see who would speak first and forfeit the fight.

If he caught half of what she'd said, and guessed at everything she hadn't, he would realize how much power he held over her. And she worried he knew her thoughts and desires better than she did herself. No man could be as in tune to a woman unless he understood the secrets she harbored deep inside.

"I'm sorry." She stepped back and shook her head. "I shouldn't have said all that."

"Yeah well, I'm pretty sure I dealt it as well as you. You make me lose control." He regarded her with those blue eyes of his. Her resolve to argue faded. "I had no control over how I lost Sam. I won't be able to live with myself if something happens to you. You're too important to risk."

BD jumped into the car, ready for the night to be over. It had barely begun. Using Maggie as bait shredded his heart with agonizingly slow slices.

He should have found a safer way to trap Adalia. Should have kissed Maggie one last time or explained more clearly why he didn't like her in Adalia's path. Should have told her exactly how important she was to him and why.

Should haves sucked stinky balls.

But by the time he'd stopped being a jerk, Craig had rushed to the door telling him they had a tip on Adalia. BD couldn't change what he'd done. All he could do was keep his promise to protect her.

"How's she holding up?"

"She's strong." *Terrified, but trying to hide it.* He leaned back against the headrest while Craig drove out of the neighborhood in a hurry for the sake of watchful eyes.

"Not what I asked."

"Your point, Oprah?"

"You care for her."

Yeah, but what difference does it make? "That isn't safe."

"She's not Sam, BD. This situation is…different."

He kept remarks to himself. What he felt for Maggie… She unearthed emotions he'd long buried. Emotions beyond passion or caring inspired by respect. Emotions he wouldn't name. "I told her."

Craig glanced his way with wide eyes. "About Sam or the baby?"

"Both." How had she gotten under his skin so quickly?

"I know what Sam meant to you better than anyone. I also see how you look at Maggie." Craig sighed with the weight of shared grief. He'd felt responsible for her death too. "You're not objective. You want to shelter her."

"Doing my job."

"Stopping Adalia is your job. Loving Maggie isn't."

"Didn't say I loved her." *Did I?*

"Didn't have to. Just…be careful."

"I know the boundaries." No friendship. No future. No nothing beyond returning to the four walls of his drab apartment.

Nope.

He would walk away, and though it would hurt, she'd be alive and never have to worry about the dangers of his job. He would never have to worry about her or her kids being caught in the crossfire.

"This is going to work." Whether trying to convince himself or Craig, BD didn't appreciate his plaintive tone. "Adalia's going to get to her one way or another. At least this way we have some control over the when and where."

Craig headed a few streets over as they'd planned. "Cap thinks it's a solid plan, and considering his military record, that's high praise."

"You think he's the one helping her?" They'd entertained the possibility briefly. Cap had the freedom to be involved, but they found no motivation.

"Cap? I hope not." Craig slipped the car into Park. "We'll know soon enough though."

Exiting the car, they checked their guns and turned toward

Maggie's. A Ford pickup swerved down the road and sped straight for the side of Craig's car. Craig rolled onto the hood. BD dove as far away from the car as possible doing a ducking roll across the grass. The truck slammed into where Craig had been standing.

The wreck was too convenient, too perfectly timed, and too much like Mike's had been to be coincidence.

BD yanked out his phone and dialed 9-1-1. Craig rushed to the driver's door where a young boy, may be fourteen, rambled in Spanish.

React faster.

Maggie was alone. Unprotected. "Craig, this is a trap."

Craig leaned into the open window of the truck. "Are you hurt? *Lastimar¿*" he translated.

BD looked from Craig to the driver to Maggie's direction, half listening while giving instructions and information to the emergency operator. His phone beeped with an incoming message.

A in kitchen.

Adalia had shown.

React faster.

BD directed to operator to dispatch Mac to Maggie's and hung up. "Hang tight, Mags. I'm coming."

"*Lastimar¿*" Craig repeated.

"No." The boy rubbed his forehead, shook his head. "No…hurt. *Estrellarse…dinero.*"

Craig opened the door and pulled the kid out. "*Estrallarse¿*"

"Auto." The boy pointed at Craig's car and slammed his hands together. "Boom. *Estrallarse.*"

"Craig." McClain was heading in, but he was too far away. Alarms rang in BD's head. His guts twisted. "Craig."

"I know." He waved a hand at BD.

"*Dinero, si¿*"

"No. Prison. Slammer." Craig pulled out his cuffs, secured one link around the boy's wrist and the other to a bar on the truck's side view mirror and ordered the kid to stay put before joining BD. "You tell dispatch where we'd be?"

"Yeah." Shoving the phone back in his pocket, he and Craig took off toward Maggie's.

His cell phone vibrated in his pocket. Running through the houses, he pulled it from his pocket to read another text from Maggie.

Someone's going to die. Depressing. Sad. Unavoidable. The certainty of the thought nagged.

Fiddling with her wedding ring, her fingers shaking more with every turn Maggie paced Jared's bedroom floor. She knew the plan. She'd fought for this, for the right to face Adalia and would see it through to the end. She'd never been more scared.

Scared of Adalia. Scared of death. Scared of losing the chance to tell Burke how she felt, how he made her tingle, how she didn't want to be without him. Ever. She wanted a relationship with him. To get past the fear of his job.

This whole warped week of dealing with Adalia's torments had driven home just how fleeting life was. No way could she allow the man who'd revealed her real self and shown her the purity of passion go without knowing her feelings.

He'd given her the strength to believe in Mike and had accepted and understood her need to be involved. Only Burke could put his need for control aside and only because he cared. But how much did he care? Enough to not bolt if she laid herself bare at his fee?

Her belly flipped at the idea.

Checking her watch, she saw he and Craig had been gone for five minutes and should be in position across the street in the neighbor's bushes. She pulled the cell from her pocket, made sure it was on silent and slipped it back. Going through the house, she flipped off lights and made a show of getting ready for bed with the darkness acting as cover to hide her moves from anyone watching.

Sometimes, being obsessive compulsive was advantageous. She knew the layout of her home, right down to the directional placement of the smallest knick-knack, in complete darkness. Shifting a few things around the house, warning signals of a sort, she prepared herself for Adalia. The activity calmed her shaking hands.

Standing in the hall by her room, satisfied with her efforts, she decided to kill time by cleaning Jared's tub. With odd luck she'd find an unidentifiable sticky substance that would require major scrubbing. The last one had resembled chocolate pudding, with the sticking power of Liquid Nails.

A soft thump, a scraping chair on the tile floor, and a curse from the kitchen signaled it was show time. A muffled crash from a few streets over ripped through the night silence. Adalia laughed.

Maggie's stomach jangled as if she'd downed a couple of energy drinks and a few caffeine pills with no food.

Breathing deep and counting to ten, she forced her heart rate to slow as she turned away from Jared's room, pulled out her phone and sent a text message to BD.

A in kitchen.

He would hurry, but she had no intention of being an easy mark. Pressing her back to the hall wall across from her room, she listened for hints as to which way Adalia headed. The living room toward her or the dining room toward BD's room?

The squeaky wheel of the antique tea cart in the dining room, the annoyance she couldn't get to stop squeaking, gave her Adalia's direction. She'd chosen to search the far side of the house first. Timing her moves with the sounds of Adalia feeling her way in the dark, Maggie stepped over the jangly metal belt she'd placed on the floor, rounded the corner into the living room, and pressed herself into the corner by the entertainment center.

The motion sensor nightlight she'd placed in BD's bathroom shined dully around the back corner of the wall blocking the view of his room from the living room. So far her little traps were working, keeping her aware of Adalia's moves. With luck, she would avoid confrontation until BD and Craig returned.

Keeping her back to the wall, Maggie slid into a squat just as Adalia stepped onto the tiled floor of the entryway. She grinned when each step the woman took made a slight sucking sound. Pouring the Sprite out and spreading it around wouldn't have done much if she hadn't worn rubber-soled shoes, but tennis were best for sneaking around.

Luck was on her side so far.

Swallowing the lump of fear in her throat, wishing her cell would vibrate with a message from BD, Maggie duck-walked across the room until she was crouching behind the love seat.

Adalia's steps became muffled by the carpet in the office. Maggie shifted around the end table she'd pulled into the walkway and hustled into the hall by BD's room. Reaching inside the doorway of his bathroom, she pulled the nightlight from the plug so as to not signal Adalia where she was, or BD when he made it back, and then she hurried through the bathroom into the bedroom.

Inhaling deeply, drawing in the spicy scent of BD and embracing the reminder of what their lovemaking had been like she wondered how much longer he would call this room his. Her home *his*.

Swallowing a chunk of fear, she grabbed the baby monitor off his bedside table, sank into the corner on the opposite side of the bed to listen to Adalia on the far side of the house, and pulled her phone out, hoping for a message from BD.

Where was he? Why hadn't he texted back? He had made a promise, but she appeared to be on her own with a killer in her home.

Sitting in BD's room by the open window, with the bed between her and the door, listening to the occasional bump on the baby monitor, she tracked Adalia's location. She cursed as she stepped on a toy truck. Just outside of Jared's room. The open doors on the bathroom connecting the kids' rooms made hearing her on the monitor easier.

Come on, BD.

Again she considered popping the window screen off and climbing out. Again she reminded herself of the plan and BD's warning. Adalia wouldn't come alone.

She needed to stay where BD expected her. At least for a little bit. And she'd promised not to call 9-1-1. As they'd discussed, they didn't know what Adalia would do if she heard sirens and they wanted to catch her partner.

"Nice painting, Sullivan." Adalia's voice, layered with menace, as she stood in Jared's room chilled Maggie more than the phone call had.

Punching buttons, Maggie sent another text, copying Craig, telling them of the traps she'd set and where she and Adalia were in the house. If they didn't show up pretty quick, she was crawling out the window and calling 9-1-1. No one had intended for her to face Adalia alone.

Where are you?

"Come out, come out wherever you are." Adalia called out from the living room. "You can't hide forever."

She's headed this way. Maggie flipped off the baby monitor and slid along the wall. Putting distance between her and the window could be a bad move, but so could keeping herself cornered. At least if she moved closer to the adjoining bathroom she had a chance of getting away. After a bracing breath she slid up the wall, slipped her phone in her pocket and promised herself she could handle this.

The hallway light flicked on. Blinking rapidly to adjust her sight, her hands shook when Adalia stepped into the doorway holding a gun at her side.

Still beautiful, but more sadistic looking than when she'd

been sentenced to life—she'd lost weight and her eyes were empty—cold and without a flicker of conscience. Prison rehabilitation had failed.

Jutting out her chin, Maggie stiffened her spine. She would not cower.

"At last, I officially meet the cherished Mrs. Sullivan." Adalia flipped on the overhead light. "Or are you hoping to make it Mrs. Harte? You've been very chummy with the detective."

"At last, I meet the cowardly Adalia Wood." Oddly, her pulse settled and her racing brain slowed. She had been *chummy* with Harte. Nothing Adalia said would defile their time together. "Hiding behind games. Too afraid to face a cop."

"Your cop can't help you now."

"I don't need a hero." *Come on, Burke. I need you!* "You might need a savior though."

"Nah. That little crash you heard has taken care of Harte and Harrison. But should they get out of it, I have another surprise for them."

Her partner. Where was he? What had she done to Burke and Craig? They couldn't be hurt. Or worse. They had to be on their way. "So you're a desperate coward unable to finish a job on your own?" That her voice sounded calm while her brain raced and her heart thundered with fear was a massive miracle.

How far could she push this? How was she going to get away?

"I saw your kid's picture." Adalia moved into the room and stood on the opposite side of the bed from Maggie. "I know you have the papers."

"That's nothing more than a pretty picture of a really cold place. And the papers are scrolls written in an ancient language. Pity Mike's dead. He could've translated them."

"Your husband had time to translate them and find out where the diamond is."

"Diamond? Why would scrolls talk about diamonds? And

neither will do you any good in hell." Maggie snapped her fingers. "Wait...there was something to do with the North Pole. I saw a movie once... The Earth is hollow and you get there by going through a portal at the North Pole. Do you believe that? Is the diamond your key?"

Laughing, Maggie scanned the room for potential weapons. Burke's laptop and the desk lamp were the closest. Not exactly something she could grab on the sly. And they weren't very effective against a gun.

"And I thought you were smart." Adalia took another step. "The papers lead to the Gryphon Diamond. It's far more valuable than any kind of science fiction crap."

"Right." *Think, Maggie. You can do this.* "What girl doesn't want an awesome diamond, but isn't the Gryphon Diamond supposed to be an extraterrestrial diamond? Doesn't that strike you as a little science fiction-like?"

"Clearly Mike translated some of the scrolls." Adalia cocked her hip and lowered the gun slightly. "That diamond is a powerful conductor."

"What are you going to conduct with it?" *Come on, BD.* Maggie relaxed a little, hoping Adalia would follow suit.

Adalia rolled her eyes. "I thought you read the papers."

"Translations of ancient languages take longer than translating something written in a currently spoken language." Maggie shrugged. "Mike didn't finish with the scrolls. I'm not exactly the expert he was."

"The diamond landed at the North Pole thousands of years ago during a meteor shower."

"So it's worth a lot of money."

"Well, yeah." Adalia waved the gun in the air as if brushing off some stupidity. "But it magnifies nuclear power by untold measures. I want to know who hid it and where."

"Oh, well since you seem to want to wipe out the world..." Maggie pointed at the bedside table. "It's in that drawer."

Adalia glanced toward the nightstand.

Did this woman really take her for an idiot? Mike hadn't finished the translation, but he'd done enough to put Maggie, BD and Craig—with the help of a few military contacts, including one of their captain's—on the right path.

The Hyperboreans had discovered an extraterrestrial diamond. A Greek god had foreseen it as a destructive force that could destroy all life, so the Hyperboreans encapsulated the stone into the heart of a Gryphon—the mythical creature of protection—statue carved from marble. Thousands of years later, the military had gotten hold of the diamond and used it during some nuclear weapons testing in the forties. The destruction during those tests had been too great, so they disposed of the diamond. Good to know Big Brother had some scruples.

They'd found nothing to tell them where it might be today. Even if Mike had translated the scrolls completely, the location wouldn't have been in them given the timeframe. The trouble lay with the secret group hunting the diamond.

"If an ancient people had this diamond," Maggie went on, "why do you think it has anything to do with nuclear power? That's not exactly something that's been around forever."

"It was like a prophecy."

"And here I thought you didn't buy into science fiction or paranormal type stuff." Gripping the laptop, prepared to hurl it at Adalia's face and end this, Maggie caught BD's spicy scent. "There's no mention of the diamond's location."

Adalia shrugged and raised her gun. "The scrolls may not tell where the diamond is now, but they will chronicle who the Hyperboreans gave it to and how to use it. I'll track it down."

"How can you know about the diamond but not know who had it?" Holding her makeshift weapon behind her back, she stepped away from the desk. Closer to the bathroom, to Adalia, and hopefully closer to BD where he would come in through the hallway.

"My grandfather told me about it." She rolled her eyes and waved her gun. "But he was out of his mind thanks to old age and disease. He said the scrolls led to the diamond."

"You need to know who it's been passed to so you can trail it to the hiding place."

A grunt behind Maggie had her turning to see a strange man—Adalia's partner—climbing in through the window. *Damn.*

Choking back fear, ignoring the slippery grip of her sweaty palms, she assured herself she could do this. Throw the computer at Adalia, dive into the windowless bathroom away from her partner, and run like hell out the other door.

"You won't have any of it," Maggie retorted. An almost silent hiss came from the bathroom beside her. BD was there. *Thank you, God!* "We've re-hidden the scrolls and the translations."

"I'm not wasting time with you."

"Give her the papers, bitch." Adalia's partner demanded. "Harte isn't here to save you this time."

Telling herself to stay calm, Maggie turned to Adalia's partner. "Tell me. What's it like?"

"What's what like?"

"Deluding yourself into thinking you're doing the right thing by helping her murder innocent people? How does it feel to know you'll never measure up to a real man?"

"That's why he drinks and beats his wife." BD stepped out of the bathroom with his weapon trained on Adalia. "It's the only way he can feel powerful. Hello, Pritchett."

BD! Yes. He'd kept his promise.

Craig stood in the hallway slightly out of Pritchett's view. His gun was trained on Adalia's back.

"You're wrong, Harte." Pritchett pulled his gun and pointed it at BD.

"I should have known you were the one helping Adalia." BD shifted his aim to Pritchett and stepped farther into the room. "I do know that while the scrolls would be a tremendous academic discovery they will remain officially undiscovered."

Keeping her gaze steady on Adalia and the weapon still

pointing at her own heart, Maggie sidled closer to BD and slightly out of the crossfire path.

Adalia and Pritchett remained oblivious to the gun pointed at the back of her head.

"You know, I've had about all the fun I can stand for one night." Maggie stepped closer still to BD. He took her hand and pulled him behind her. Now he had Pritchett and Adalia's guns trained on him.

Adalia took a step closer and pointed the gun at BD's forehead. Pritchett lowered his to BD's chest. Maggie's heart slammed her ribs with knowledge. He wouldn't survive this.

She widened her eyes and stared over Adalia's shoulder at Craig. *Do something!* Craig stood frozen. Unmoving. Unreadable.

"Mags, bathroom." Totally grateful to have BD there to be demanding and arrogant, she wasn't able to obey. She'd claimed she didn't need a hero, but as he backed her toward the bathroom she loved knowing she had one.

"Oh, screw this," Pritchett sneered.

In surreal slow motion, he and BD squeezed their triggers. Five pops resounded through the room followed by two more. BD jerked backward knocking Maggie into the bathroom.

Blood splattered her face. She screamed. Burke stumbled and took her to the floor. Two other thuds hit the floor—one in the bedroom, one in the hall beyond—before a buzzing silence reigned.

Maggie struggled to get out from under Burke. Her slamming heart plummeted at the sight of his blood covering his shirt.

"Mags." He tried to push her back, but his hands fell away.

Craig leapt to Adalia's side and kicked her gun away. Pritchett came into the bathroom. Craig was on his heels. Tense, but otherwise stone-faced. "They're dead."

"Good." Burke's voice, raspy and strained, was followed by a gasp.

Hot tears rolled down Maggie's face as she knelt at his

side. Blood poured from his shoulder, staining his shirt and the white carpet.

"We need to move him to the bedroom so we have more room to work." Craig reached for him. "You with me, BD?"

"Yeah."

After thirty seconds of cussing, groaning and more bleeding, Craig and Pritchett had Burke on the bedroom floor. Maggie focused her vision on him, trying to block the other two bodies from her peripheral.

"I'll deal with the bodies," Pritchett said.

"Bodies?" Burke's voice was fading with his color.

"It was Cap," Craig said. "He stopped the dispatcher from calling Mac."

"Craig, towels." She couldn't care about who lay in her hall or other details with Burke bleeding in her arms. He couldn't die. "Burke, stay with me."

"Ambulance."

"I know." She pushed a hand against the chest wound and grabbed her phone with the other to dial 9-1-1. He'd be fine. He had to be fine. She pushed on his chest to stop the blood flow and propped the phone between her ear and shoulder. He moved away from the pain. "Damn it! Don't move. You'll be all right."

The seconds of waiting for a dispatcher to pick up dragged like hours. Burke was going to bleed to death if they didn't answer.

"Mags…safe."

Her throat closed. Her stomach and chest lurched with the effort to breathe. *Stop it!* She ordered herself to calm down before she hyperventilated. He'd been shot, but all he worried about was her safety.

"I'm here. Shh." Apparently taking her at her word, he passed out.

"9-1-1. What's your emergency?" He was still alive. He wasn't going to die.

"An officer's been shot. In the chest near his left

shoulder." Craig stepped up beside her. She yanked the towel from him and shoved it against Burke's chest. She would *not* break down now.

"Ma'am, what's your address? I'll get you help."

She rattled off her address.

"How much blood has he lost?"

"I'm not exactly measuring it. He's as white as my carpet was." Belatedly, she remembered the speaker feature on the phone and, after pushing the button, laid it on the floor. With both hands free she could be more help.

The dispatcher's irritatingly calm voice sounded tinny over the speaker as he repeated questions and instructions.

"Maggie, you're shaking too badly. Let me." Craig covered her hand, applied steady pressure to Burke's chest, and handed her a smaller towel to wipe her hands off. Keeping pressure on Burke's chest, he took over dealing with the operator.

She pushed Burke's hair off his forehead, worried at how white his normally tan skin was turning. The metallic stench of the blood, the slickness of his life on her hands and splattered on her face, threatened to take her out.

Swallowing the rising bile, she ran her hands over the man she loved. He'd ended the threats she'd faced, but he'd risked his own life. It had likely been a replay of the scene with Samantha, only he was the one with the bullet.

Sirens sounded nearby. He paled more. His breathing grew shallower with each dragging minute.

"Stay with me, Burke." She brushed the hair away from his forehead and leaned close, resting her cheek on his. He was passed out, but she couldn't stop talking. She whispered in his ear, hoping he could hear her. "The ambulance is close. You'll be fine."

"He'll beat this, Maggie." Craig met her gaze over Burke, each of them doing their best to comfort him and prevent too much blood loss. "Stay strong."

"How can you know that? This is *not* okay. He has a bullet

in him."

"It's not the first time. And he has too much to live for."

In a flurry of movement, a group of men crowded the bedroom, efficiently moving her away from Burke, so she was forced to watch from the side. When they lifted him on the stretcher, he moaned. She dived back to him. Ignoring their insistence she stay back, she grabbed his hand, assuring herself he could feel her.

He would survive.

"Ma'am, you need to move back," an EMT said.

Her eyes flashed to his.

He waved a hand in surrender. "Or not."

"Hurts like hell." Burke's slurred voice had her whipping her face to his.

"I know, baby. Stay with me."

He groaned and slid back under. She followed the EMTs as they wheeled her wounded hero to the ambulance. His lashes rested lifelessly against his cheeks. Her tongue thickened. She couldn't swallow or get air.

He had to be okay. Her heart beat twice its normal speed. The throb of each pulse point drummed in her ears. His blood stained her hands.

Cold. She was so cold. She couldn't see another man she loved die.

Chapter Thirteen

Maggie twisted her wedding ring around her finger and paced the overly disinfected floor, waiting for an update on Burke's surgery. Whispers floated eerily down the hall, but once the nurses and doctors had given her clean scrubs to change into, finished poking at her, and asking annoying questions, no one else had spoken to her.

Craig and had stayed at the house to deal with Adalia and their captain. Maggie had called her parents and Grace before they could hear the story on the news and after assuring them she was fine, she begged them not to come to the hospital. She needed to be alone for a while.

She looked down at Burke's blood staining her cuticles and broke into fresh sobs. Dropping onto a chair, she covered her face with her hands. Why wouldn't someone come tell her something? Anything? What was taking so long?

"Maggie, don't take this the wrong way, but you look like hell."

She jumped up to see Craig watching her. She hadn't expected to see him so soon.

"Have you heard anything?" She squeezed the bridge of her nose. The pressure that had been building all night refused to ease off. She had to hold it together. She couldn't fall apart again until she was alone and knew Burke was recovering. "No one's talking to me."

He stepped in her path and put his hands on her shoulders. "He'll be all right."

"Can you guarantee me that? Can you give me a one-hundred-percent guarantee he'll be okay?"

"Yes." Craig kissed her cheek.

"I'm not so sure." When she'd pressed her hands against Burke's chest, stopping his blood from spilling out, she'd been useful. Now, the doctors and nurses cared for him. Her only purpose was to fiddle her hands and wait.

"He's lucky to have you, Maggie."

"But I don't have him."

"Not true."

"How? He's lying on an operating table with a bullet in his chest because of me."

"He's going to run faster than ever when he's healed. Maggie." Craig took her hand and led her to a chair in the corner. "If you'd seen him trying to get to you after your texts you wouldn't have a doubt."

Calming enough to think, she remembered the crash and Adalia's laughing taunts about it. "Adalia did something to hold you two up. What?"

"She paid a teenager to crash into the car."

"Holy shit!"

"We were already out. As you can see we weren't hurt and it only slowed BD down long enough for him to call it in." Craig leaned forward, braced his elbows on his knees, and sighed. "I've known him all my life, but I've never seen him this way. Not even with Sam."

"You knew her well?"

"She was my sister. He and Sam loved each other like crazy." Craig turned his head and looked at her. Sadness clouded his eyes. "But Maggie, he adores you. He would cut his arm off if it was necessary to protect you. And don't get me started on what your kids do to him."

She creased her brow and studied Craig. As kind as he was he would never compare to the man she now thought of when she woke up and before she fell asleep.

Only Burke could claim the part of her heart she'd thought would be impossible to give away again. The giving hadn't been her choice to give it away, but it would be her choice whether or not she admitted it. "Do you mean that?"

"Yes. So when he gets out of here I hope you'll think about giving him a chance without the secrets in the way."

Craig sat with her until he got called back to the station,

leaving her alone in the waiting room. Though Pritchett had helped stop Adalia he'd apparently shifted back to useless cop mode and was leaving details and follow-ups to Craig. And like Craig said, he'd been the one to shoot Captain Winchester. He'd have to face the resulting headaches.

Burke had been in surgery for nearly three hours when a sweet-looking, older couple came in and sat in another corner about an hour ago. They held hands and leaned against one another, but never said a word. She might've asked why they were there, if the new foundation of her world wasn't shaking.

The interminable waiting grated her nerves quicker than an electric meat grinder. What could be taking so long? Why weren't they finished yet?

She alternated between pacing and sitting, twisting her ring the whole time. She'd thought about going for a drink, but didn't want to leave the room and risk missing the doctor.

Not that they seemed concerned about her fear growing with each minute. Yeah okay, so their attention was good for BD, but it sucked for her.

"Young lady," the older man said, "whatever it is, pacing won't make it better."

The man she loved was having a bullet dug out of his chest and some stranger wanted her to sit still? She started to give him her opinion, but bit back her nasty remark since they more than likely didn't come to the hospital in the middle of the night for a good time. "Forgive me."

She sat and fidgeted with her ring. Her knees bounced. Her skin crawled as images of Burke bleeding on her floor flashed in her mind. Shaking her head, she tried to dislodge the image. It wouldn't budge. The sight of his blood still on her hands brought it all back.

Come on, Burke. As if he could hear her thoughts, she cried out to him in her mind. *You have to get through this. I need you.*

"Is your husband here?"

Maggie shook her head at the woman's question, but

couldn't sit still. Lurching from her seat, she straightened the chairs and magazines on the tables she'd already straightened several times. "My husband's dead."

"I'm sorry." The woman's blue eyes glittered with sadness as she moved toward Maggie. She had a kind face, but Maggie wasn't interested in chit chat. "I know how hard it is to lose someone you love."

Maggie gripped the back of a chair until her knuckles turned white. She'd lost her husband and Burke's life lingered in jeopardy. She pointed to the man gripping the woman's hand. "That your husband?"

"For fifty years next month." Pride and love shone in her eyes.

"Then you don't know what I've lost." *Or stand to lose again.* Maggie swiped at the tears rolling down her cheeks.

"I have a pretty good idea." The woman slid her arm around Maggie's waist and led her to a chair. "My son lost his wife a couple of years ago. I watched grief rip at him the way fear's ripping through you now."

Maggie choked back her tears and studied the woman. Her tender touch sent familiar warmth through Maggie's heart. Familiar cobalt eyes met her own. "You're Burke's mom."

Surprise flickered in her eyes. "You know my son?"

Maggie found herself regaining the control she'd felt slipping further and further from her grasp. "He moved into my house last weekend."

"Maggie." The woman squeezed her hand. Pleasure, despite the circumstances, lit up her face. "I'm Sydney Harte. My husband, Tommy."

The man moved to sit on the other side of Maggie. His smile soothed her nerves as easily as Burke's could. "I wish I could've met you under better circumstances, but I'm glad you're here for him."

"Tell me, Mrs. Sullivan." Tommy sat back and smiled. "Do you know how BD got shot? We haven't been able to talk to Craig long enough for details."

Her heart clutched. These people loved Burke. As nice as they seemed to be, they wouldn't welcome her after hearing what role she'd played in his ending up in an operating room. So fine. She'd see for herself he was recovering and leave them alone.

"Yes." She ignored her fear and told them about Adalia. The more she talked about it, about the time spent with Burke, the more she relaxed. The image of him bleeding on her floor receded to the background. Images of the ways he'd kissed her, made love to her and taunted her to keep her distracted from the crap going on around her moved to the forefront. He'd been her hero from the start.

A doctor dressed in blue scrubs, a paper hat and shoe covers stepped into the room and ambled toward them. Exhaustion stamped his face. Her heart rate kicked up.

Sydney and Tommy stood as a unit, obviously ready for whatever news they would hear. Maggie moved to the side, keeping enough distance between herself and Burke's family to be reminded she wasn't a part of the inner circle. They mattered most.

Sydney turned and reached a hand out to her. A simple gesture from a virtual stranger erased her loneliness. Swallowing another wave of tears struggling to break free, she stepped forward to join his parents. No wonder she'd fallen in love with Burke.

The doctor pulled his scrub cap off his head. His kind brown eyes were pinched with fatigue. "BD's in recovery and will be moved to a room shortly. He'll be with us for a few days, but he'll be fine."

"How much damage?" Tommy asked.

"The bullet punctured a lung. He'll have a chest tube while that heals. It missed his ribs, but we had to sew some muscle back together."

Tommy continued asking the doctor questions. Burke's parents had been kind to include her, but she needed out. Now. Ignoring the tension building in her neck and shoulders,

Maggie eased out of the room. Just a quick peek to see for herself he was okay and she'd be out of their way.

She rounded a corner and ran into a young nurse. Maggie forced a smile she didn't feel, nodded politely, and headed toward the recovery room. Stepping into a large room, she saw several empty beds. Burke lay in one close to the door. Covering her mouth, she stood at the end of his bed and let the relief he was alive wash over her.

His skin was almost as pale as the sheets, but he had more color than he had while lying on her floor. Tubes running from his chest and arms were taped to his skin. A monitor beside the bed beeped and showed his vitals. He looked like hell, but he was breathing and slept peacefully thanks to meds. That's all that mattered.

Moving to his side, careful not to touch any of the tubes sticking out of him, she brushed a kiss to his lips. "I love you, Burke. More than I thought possible."

BD dreamt of Maggie bent over him, saying she loved him, asking him to stay with her. Somewhere in the midst of all the pain and disjointed sounds and smells of the hospital he'd been enveloped by the warm scent of vanilla. The brush of her lips on his hadn't been imagined. The jolt of awareness that had shot through his achy body had been real. He'd just been unable to move, open his eyes, or speak.

Now, he had nothing but time on his hands. Time he spent sleeping, trying to convince his family he was all right, and torturing himself with the memory of Maggie.

She had grabbed his interest and captured his heart before he could stop her. She'd been at the hospital during his surgery, but had stayed away since. Why? Did she plan on coming back?

He wanted to yank the tube out of his chest and go find the answers for himself. An attempt to sit up in bed had his chest burning until he admitted defeat and slumped back. Damn

Adalia.

"You know, Detective Harte. You'll heal faster if you stop moving so much."

He shrugged at his nurse. Then he winced, because as usual he moved the wrong shoulder. Beth Sanders was cute, something men in hospital beds wanted, but he only wanted to see one woman. "The walls start to close in on you after awhile. Even the windows don't help."

"Perhaps knowing you're being released tomorrow will?" She moved to his side and helped him adjust the pillows behind him. "Better?"

He nodded. "What time?"

"We'll get the tubes off you this afternoon. If all goes well the paperwork should be ready in the morning."

"Good." With a light at the end of the tunnel he could plan his attack on Maggie.

She wasn't going to get away with invading every square inch of him, turning him inside out, and then walking away. He'd given up on his happily ever after and stopped reaching out to people. She'd shown him he couldn't stop living and fighting.

"Now rest." Beth jotted notes on his chart and headed for the door. "Visiting hours start soon and I'm sure your family will break the rules on the number of visitors."

He settled back against the pillows, knowing she hadn't really tried to enforce the rule. It wouldn't have held up against his parents, Craig, his sister Laurel and her husband John. The downer of their visits was they couldn't bring his niece. He missed seeing her.

A short time later as Beth predicted, the crew that was his family showed up to crowd his room again and keep his mind occupied. Searching their faces as they came in, he missed the face of the woman who'd captured his heart, and terrified him to the bone with her courage.

"If I didn't know better," Laurel said with a smirk, "I'd think you didn't like me. You always frown when we come in."

"Sorry. I was sort of hoping to see someone else." Or that he could escape the four walls and medical chains of his prison. He adored his sister, but hers wasn't the face he needed to see.

Splitting up, his mom took one side of the bed and Laurel claimed the other. His dad and John nodded and settled in the two chairs in the room. They'd settled into the routine the first day of letting Mom and Laurel fuss while they watched whatever he had the TV tuned to, and that was never exciting because he didn't give a damn about anything on TV.

"I think," Mom said, "he's waiting for a beautiful woman to come kiss his wounds."

His mind perked. Alert. Hopeful. Had they talked to Maggie? Did they know why she was staying away? "I wouldn't complain. Do you have one in mind?"

"Your nurse is cute enough," Dad put in.

"A little young I think." Not to mention he apparently liked them with an edge of temper these days.

"Young's good, she'll have lots of energy."

"I might consider her if she'd let me have some decent food." Or if she aroused him by walking in a room. Forming a plan, knowing he needed his dad's help with the first phase, he winced as he looked between his mom and Laurel. "This hospital crap blows."

"You rest." Mom brushed her hand over his arm.

"We'll go get you something," Laurel said. "John, you have the keys?"

"Yeah," John grinned and rolled his eyes behind Laurel. His brother-in-law made his sister happy with his quiet support, and he had an uncanny way of knowing what people needed. "I'll drive."

Dad chuckled after everyone left. "It isn't nice to use their concern."

"They'll forgive me."

"That they will." Dad moved to sit on the foot of the bed. "So what's up?"

196

"I need you to go to the bank for me."

Dad stroked his chin like he always did when he suspected something. "You going to do some shopping in here?"

"I need Granny's ring from my safe deposit box. You're on the list to be granted access."

"Would this have anything to do with a lovely young woman with brown hair and chocolate eyes?"

"You've seen Maggie?" Forgetting his pain, he straightened in the bed. "Was she here? What'd she say? How did she look?"

Dad laughed and pushed him back down. "She was in the waiting room while you were in surgery. She left when she heard you were all right."

And hadn't been back, but he'd swear he heard her say she loved him. The pain meds they had him on didn't cause hallucinations. She had to be real. "How did she look?"

"Scared and worried. Tell me about her."

"She's…" The words he needed escaped him. He couldn't think of a way to do her justice. She'd been in his soul, her face, her soft touch, her encouraging voice, giving him a reason to fight back when his body begged him to let go. "She rescued me from a depressing life by showing me there are still things worth fighting for. I'm going to ask her to marry me."

"Really? What happened to your vow never to love again? And Craig mentioned she has kids."

"She's it for me. And her kids." BD relaxed deeper into the bed knowing she was okay. "I'm a lot of things, but I'm not stupid. I can't let her go without a fight."

"Your mother and sister will be thrilled. I liked her."

"I love her." He rubbed his fingers over his lips, sure the memory of her touch made them tingle again.

"I'll get you the ring before we leave town."

"You're going home?"

"We have to. I have a court case I can't miss, and John needs to get back to his clients."

"The day's work for a judge." Missing his family even

before they left, BD sighed. "One last favor, Dad. Don't mention this to anyone just yet. Maggie's had a rough road and may take some convincing."

He hadn't given her any reason to think he would stick around when the case was over. And with the way he'd treated her at times, he no doubt had a lot of work to do to make things right with her. He would start as soon as he got out of this bed and found a way to make her listen.

Maggie turned the car off and rested her head on the steering wheel. She doubted the country air would do much to clear her confusion, but she'd needed to escape. The farm was the first place to come to mind.

Walking to the tree where her favorite bench now sat in shambles, she saw the lights at her parents' home. They'd be settling in with a bowl of popcorn to watch the news as if the depressing broadcast was great entertainment. They were weird at times, but they were a team who faced everything together. She wanted that.

Sitting on the ground with one of the bench legs across her lap, breathing in the night air, she thought about the last year. Everything she and her kids had been through. The things she'd learned about herself, including the new inner strength she'd come to recognize.

In the moonlight shining through the tree branches, she rubbed the ring on her finger. "Oh, Mike. Moving on shouldn't hurt this bad. But I fell in love with a man who risks his life every day, and that scares me."

For the first time in her life, she felt completely alone. No one would tell her what to do this time. Breathing deeply, she fought back the tears and refused to feel sorry for herself. She was a big girl and could make her own decisions. "How am I supposed to deal with this? What if I lose him like I lost you?"

"Does he ever answer?"

Jumping at the hushed sound of her dad's voice, she

looked up with her hand on her chest. "Sheesh, Dad. Do you have to sneak around?"

"I'm not the one coming onto the property at night without calling first." He sat down and wrapped an arm around her shoulders. "What are you doing here?"

"Thinking."

She'd sat here with her dad after Mike had died. He'd listened silently while she told him about the accident and all her fears of the future. Thinking back on it, she felt more like crying now than she had then—because she realized how much Burke had changed her from the first moment.

She hadn't needed to cry over Mike once Burke had let her weep. His tenderness had helped her find the control she'd needed to survive. Then he'd shown back up and made her want things she'd never believed existed, and was afraid to hope she could have.

"What's going on, Maggie?"

"Burke gets out of the hospital in the morning."

"I heard." Dad laid his cheek on her head and squeezed her close. "That's good."

"Yeah, I guess."

Rubbing her arms, he gave her the comfort he'd always offered. "You're scared of loving him."

She closed her eyes and willed the tears not to fall. She sniffled when they did anyway. "This was all just another day on the job for him. I don't even know if he intends to come back."

"Maggie."

She laughed despite her mood. Good ole Dan Malone, always able to pin her thoughts without an effort and call her bullshit with one heavily toned word. She never stood a chance of hiding things from him, had given up most of her attempts years ago.

He sat her away, grabbed her chin and then made her look at him. "Stop doubting yourself and BD. What you could have together."

"I'm…"

"Scared. Worried about getting close and losing him." Dad kissed her nose. "And you worry about your kids and how they'll adjust if he stays."

"Yeah." Unable to sit, Maggie rose and walked a few feet away. She stood a good chance of having to live without Burke. If not now, then at any time because of his job.

"What do you see when you look in BD's eyes? How did you feel when you were with him?"

She thought about how to put her answer into words. "I feel safe and special. I'd like to think I see the future."

"Then you can't live in fear of what *might* happen." He moved to her, placed his hands on her shoulders, and turned her toward him. "Only you can decide if he's the right choice for you. And yes, a life with him will be tough at times because of his job. You've already lived through some heavy stuff with him."

"So am I supposed to pretend his work doesn't bother me?"

"No. If he's the right man, you owe it to him to shoot straight. Trust him."

There'd been a lot of discussions about trust with him. "Why can't I find a man like you? One without a dangerous job?"

"You had that. Mike's job is not what kept him safe, and Burke's isn't necessarily what he'll die from. Life happens with or without us. It guarantees us nothing."

"That doesn't help me much." She had more questions than answers. Dad always had a strange way of helping.

"Then ask yourself how much he means to you. Think about what your life was like without him, and how it might be with him. And know whatever you decide, we *all* approve." He kissed her forehead before walking away.

A tear slid down her cheek as she watched her dad disappear in the darkness. Even if she could accept Burke's job, nothing said he wanted a long-term relationship with her.

He was a special man, and though he tried so hard at times to be an arrogant jerk, deep down he was kind. Hot. Passionate. Amazing in so many ways.

He hadn't even seemed to think she was crazy for the way she attacked the bushes in the yard. And he hadn't tried to take over the job. He understood her.

She hadn't known him long, but did it really matter? Wasn't it more important to treasure the good things he gave her and enjoy whatever time she could have with him?

What she had with Mike had been good, but she wanted to spend the rest of her life with someone different. A man who gave her everything she'd ever wanted. A man who could rescue her heart, as well as her life.

Chapter Fourteen

Maggie fisted her hand at her side until her nails dug into her palm. *Get it together. He isn't going to bite.*

"Can I help you?"

She turned and smiled at the young nurse, Beth Sanders according to her name badge. Pointing at the door to Burke's room, she realized how idiotic she must look. "I'm his ride."

"I can promise in his current state, you have the advantage."

Doubtful. "Is he okay to be leaving today? Should he stay longer?"

The nurse shook her head and held up the papers in her hand. "The doctor signed the release papers."

Maggie held her hand out and smiled. "Do you mind if I give those to him?"

Nurse Sanders handed her the papers, but didn't release them instantly. "Take care of him."

Maggie looked in the other woman's eyes and saw her interest in Burke went deeper than concern for a patient. Poor girl would be toast if he'd even hinted at a return interest. He'd better not have.

"Promise." She took the papers and pushed the door to Burke's room open.

Pacing the floor, he spun and stared at her. Silence charged the room as their eyes locked.

The silence bellowed.

"Hi," she finally managed. She wanted to rush across the room and throw herself at him, but needed to take this slow. Unsure of herself, she leaned against the door.

His mouth slowly raised into a smile. His steady gaze seared her soul, filling her with the warmth she'd been missing the last three days.

"Mags," his sex-dipped voice rasped.

She could do this.

He held out his right hand and raised a brow in challenge. When she got close enough, he took her hand in his, and linked their fingers. Tugging her closer, he pulled her hand to his lips. The kiss he brushed across her knuckles sent shivers of excitement coursing over her. His lids drooped. How had she stayed away?

"I've missed you, Mags."

She closed her eyes as the lingering tension drained from her shoulders. He did care. With a deep breath, she opened her eyes and smiled. "Are you okay?"

He tugged her until she was pressed against his right side. "Better now that you're here."

"I mean your wound." She tried not to move too much as she curled into him. She didn't want to jar him, but staying away wasn't possible.

"I know what you meant." He ran his thumb in small circles over her knuckles. "I'm fine as long as I don't breathe wrong or move too fast, but I'm not going to break if you touch me."

She rested her free hand on his chest and felt the steady beat of his heart. Strength and warmth radiated off him. She grew more certain by the second he would in fact be okay, but it didn't stop her worrying.

Pulling away from him, she picked up his bag. "Come on, I'll take you home."

"Where's home?"

"You're stuff is still in your room at my place."

They didn't talk much during the ride home. She wasn't sure where to start and she didn't want to be trapped in the car if it didn't go the way she hoped. She carried his bag into the kitchen and sat it on the table. "Would you like something to eat? You've got to be tired of hospital food?"

"What did you have in mind?"

"I could cook." She went to the fridge and pulled open the double doors. The cool air soothed her heated cheeks some.

She wasn't handling this well. "There's ice cream."

He stayed silent until she turned. His blue gaze arrested her. "You have chocolate sauce?"

"Yeah." Her heart pounded, her blood thrummed and her body shook with each breath. "Sit down and I'll get the stuff."

"I can help." He went to the cabinets and got bowls and spoons. As he passed behind her, he rubbed his hand along her lower back.

She sighed.

The man fit her. He enjoyed her family, her kids. He gave her screaming passion that singed her skin hours later. He might be abrasive at times, but he'd offered her the security she needed to break down and face the fact she couldn't handle everything on her own all the time. He'd given her the security to know she didn't have to be strong every minute of every day.

Turning to place the ice cream and toppings on the island, she slammed into his chest. "Sorry."

His hands rested on her shoulders, his fingers rubbing the line of her collar bone. "Don't be. I like the feel of you."

What's a woman supposed to say to that? "Thank you, I think."

He narrowed his eyes and studied her face. "You're smiling."

"You've seen me smile."

"It's in your eyes this time. The shadows of fear and sadness are gone." He leaned back and looked her up and down. "You're wearing jeans and a T-shirt. You're hair is in a ponytail. Hot pink flip-flops."

"So?"

"You were dressed like this with hot pink cleaning gloves the first day I came here. Casual. Comfortable."

"And?" What was he getting at? And how did he remember what she'd worn a year ago?

"You're happy and relaxed instead of feeling like you have to be in complete control. It suits you."

"You and Craig killed my problems." She stepped back and moved around him. He was entirely too perceptive.

"Right." His voice dropped an octave.

He slanted a glance her way that slid over her skin as gentle as a touch. Her stomach jumped. *Calm down, Maggie.* Popping the top of the whipped cream, she shook the can, and lifted it to her mouth.

Grinning, a wicked glint in his gaze, he leaned against the counter. "Are you sure that's a good idea?"

"What?"

"You dug pretty far back for that. How long's it been in there?"

"It's canned air. It doesn't go bad."

"It has a date on it." He took the can from her and shook it slowly. "I think it should be tested."

"Tested?" Had he lost his mind?

His cobalt stare was captivating as he shifted away from the counter. She turned to stay facing him. Like a slow dance, he maneuvered her so her back was against the island. Was he flirting with her?

Her pulse drummed in her ears. Lighting quick flashes of heat struck her body, leaving a tingle of awareness behind. "Harte."

"I think I need to make sure it's still…edible."

Daaaang. He looked as hungry as when he'd stood before her holding a condom. Like he could, would, devour her in an instant.

"It was good last time." The flare of arousal in his eyes broadcast her mistake.

He stepped closer, effectively pinning her to the counter without touching her. "I remember."

And I want more! She pressed the mute button on the voice in her head, but it didn't help to suppress the arousal begging her to take anything he offered. "Harte."

"I thought you wanted some."

"Umm." *Distance. Must have distance.* She slid along the

counter. They needed to talk. She couldn't even think.

He edged along in front of her. "I'll take that as a yes."

Allowing her no argument, not that she had a good one, he yanked her against his good side and locked an arm around her waist, imprisoning her against his hard, extremely aroused body.

"You know…"

"How good you're going to taste? Yes." His sexy I-know-how-to-make-you-shiver rumble rippled across her nerves.

He aimed the whipped cream can at her face. His huge body, pressed against hers, radiated heat. He was after sex, and as dangerous as the idea was, she couldn't make herself try to step away.

She wanted whatever he wanted to give her. For however long she could have it.

"I suggest you open up, Mags. This could get messy."

Her eyes locked with his. The breath backed up in her lungs, her body hummed. The body bliss he'd brushed over her earlier wouldn't be the same. His earlier patience was snapping to get free.

She wanted to know how his unleashed desire tasted. Without blinking, she licked her lips and opened her mouth.

"You're going to melt faster than the ice cream." His smile was wickedly sexy, as he filled her mouth with cream. A heartbeat later, he dipped his head and covered her open mouth with his.

His tongue curved into her mouth and drew some of the cream into his own. He drew back a few inches and licked his lips as if to savor the taste. His hands gripped her hips and held her tight against his arousal.

Her stomach clenched. She swelled and ached for his touch. To feel his mouth on her like before. To feel him lap at her the way he was lapping at the cream in her mouth.

Melt? No, she was evaporating.

He lowered his head a second time. His unwavering gaze promised explosive pleasures. She trembled beneath him. His breath teased her lips as he traced her lower one with his fingers and smiled.

He dipped a fingertip in the quickly dissolving pile of cream in her mouth. Licking it clean, he sighed. "So creamy."

Certain he was going to repeat the embellished torment until he'd emptied her, she was surprised when he slid his tongue in her mouth and finished off the cream in one lick. Then, he took her mouth in a hard, hot, fast kiss.

His hips ground into hers. She slid a leg up his, trying to get closer. Her heart slammed against her ribs, pumping boiling blood through her veins. The lace of her bra scraped across her sensitized nipples like coarse sandpaper. Her knee buckled. She grabbed Burke for support.

With a smile, he grabbed her hips and lifted her to the island. She helped by jumping so he didn't hurt himself. His fingers dug into her scalp and pulled her head back. His teeth nipped at her bared throat. She moaned, locked her ankles behind him, and pushed into his erection.

"I want you naked."

She nodded.

"Here. On the counter." He slid his tongue over the edge of her ear. "So I can eat these toppings off you instead of the ice cream."

Reaching for his back, she found the hem of his shirt and pulled it over his head, careful of his injury. He could eat all he wanted later. She wanted him. Now.

"In a hurry, Mags?"

"Yes." She brushed her hand along the edge of the bandage. He stiffened against her, but relaxed when she smiled.

His thumb brushed a path along her hairline. "You…"

She buried her fingers in his thick hair and yanked his mouth to hers. What was with him? He was all over the fast and furious moves until it came to doing the deed. Then he turned all soft and tender.

Well, forget it. She'd had years of soft and tender. Boring! She wanted flames and dynamite. She wanted them from him.

He pulled back and stared into her eyes as his chest heaved. "You're still dressed."

"Then quit wasting time." Because if he didn't finish her off pretty quick she was going to knock him on his butt and take over.

"Mags, I—"

"Need to shut up and keep your promises." She popped her hips off the counter and bumped his erection.

He sucked a breath through his teeth.

Pulling back a bit, she reached for the snap of his jeans and shoved them past his bulging erection. Looking at him the first time she'd thought he would be too big, but he filled her perfectly. She wanted him buried deep. Now.

He finally pulled her up enough to yank her shirt off. Her bra disappeared with it. His mouth closed over her breast while his busy fingers pulled at her pants.

"You taste like warm vanilla. And cream."

She buried a hand in his hair and held him close. The flames surging through her thrilled her more than a free fall from an airplane. The room spun when he yanked her hips to the edge and buried himself in her.

"Burke!"

"That's right." He thrust into her again and again, grinding himself against her clit each time. "Scream it all you want. No one can hear you, and no one is going to stop you."

Completely out of control and loving it, she writhed. Feeling completely wanton, she reveled in the experience of being taken on the kitchen counter.

Her heart stumbled in her chest as he collapsed onto her. His head rested between her breasts. His heart slammed against her stomach. Next time they'd go to her room, because she planned to enjoy him as long as possible.

"Crap." He lurched away from her and grabbed his pants.

Stunned, and brain fogged, she pushed up on her elbows. He yanked up his pants and grabbed for his shirt. "Burke?"

"Stupid. Sorry." He muttered and mumbled as he picked

up her clothes and tossed them to her.

"What's wrong?" Other than the orgasmic hit-and-run? She'd wanted to see him out of control and she had, but his reaction was way stronger than necessary.

He smacked his hand against his forehead and backed away. "We shouldn't have done this. This was wrong on so many levels."

His words lashed out and cooled her roaring emotions more effectively than a bucket of ice water in the face. Jumping off the counter, she grabbed the waist of his pants before he retreated. "Hold it. What is wrong with what we just did?"

He looked toward the ceiling. "Put some clothes on."

"No." She took his chin in her hand and forced him to look at her. "Tell me what your problem is. You can't take something beautiful and fulfilling and turn it into a mistake that fast."

He'd granted another fantasy. He'd treated her like a woman he couldn't do without. Like a desirable woman capable and worthy of fiery passion. The kind she didn't want to be without.

"We didn't use a condom. We aren't in—"

"A relationship?" She indicated her naked body and locked her eyes with his. "I disagree, and for what it's worth I'm on the pill to regulate my cycles."

"Oh, um…"

Now it was his turn to be speechless. That was new for him, but would work for her. She wanted some answers. "How often does this happen? You getting shot or hurt on the job?"

"This is the second time in over ten years. Craig and I are good at our jobs, and we're careful. Why? Don't you want to put some clothes on?"

"No. It wouldn't change my vulnerability." Life had no guarantees. "And, I like to know what I'm getting into."

"Getting into?"

"I don't know how to do this, Burke." She yanked her ponytail out and fisted her hair. "I don't know if I'm strong enough."

"Do what?" He angled his head. Slowly, a smile spread across his mouth and lit his eyes. "Forget that. Do you trust me?"

"I do. I also worry about you."

"Then we're on the same wavelength." He tugged her hand to his lips like he had in the hospital. "I'm sorry. Sorry for any lies or hurt feelings. Sorry for scaring you, though I can't say it'll be the last time."

Sighing, she moved into him and wrapped her arms around his waist. His combination of tenderness and strength amazed her. His size alone made her feel feminine. Protected. His tenderness made her feel cherished. "Why does it seem you understand me better than anyone ever has?"

"I get everything about you, Mags." He pulled back and kissed her softly on the lips. Then at the corner of each eye and on the tip of her nose. "You slipped under my skin from the beginning. And when you worked that punching bag…" He sighed with a goofy smile. "That's when I think you first stole a piece of my heart. You make me happy. You're in my pores."

"Does that bother you?"

"Not as much as I thought it should. You rescued me from a darkness I hadn't realized I was living in."

Her heart sighed. As cliché as it sounded, she'd swear it was a sigh.

"Burke." He had his moods, but she'd stopped thinking of him as the arrogant Harte. He would forever be Burke to her. "I want to see where we can take this."

"Do you mean that?"

Wincing when he moved his left shoulder the wrong way, BD blew out a breath and linked their fingers. She couldn't make a statement like that and not answer him, but she wasn't talking. "Mags, I'm sorry you were scared. I care about you more than you can imagine."

"I'm glad." Her eyes widened. Her tongue swept across her lips.

"I'd like to see how far we can take this." He leaned forward until his face was close to hers. "Maybe try it out for say the next fifty or sixty years."

"I…you…"

He grinned as his always confident Maggie stammered. "You what?"

"Most men don't deal well with long-term commitments. Especially with single moms."

"You're right." He narrowed his eyes. "Let me try again."

"Harte."

"I thought you'd started calling me Burke, which I really like by the way." He locked his gaze with hers and saw everything he could ever hope to have. Love, fiery passion, a few great kids were only the beginning. "That's okay. I can do better."

"Don't…"

"No. Too late." He walked to the bag she'd put on the table and grabbed a small box from a side pocket. He went back to her, where she still stood completely and gloriously naked.

Maybe one day he'd tell her how her serious don't-you-think-about-doing-that tone turned him on. Much later. A man needed some secrets. "Listen close, Mags. I'm only saying this once, and I hope you're not in an arguing mood."

"Burke."

"Better." He grinned. "The time alone with you has been beyond amazing, if challenging at times, but I love being with you and your kids."

She chewed on her bottom lip. The soft flesh would plump up and taste heavenly when he finally kissed her again.

"Mags." He leaned back a little. Space and less touching would help focus. She muddled his brain when she got too close. "I never thought I'd be doing this with you naked."

"Burke, are you…"

"Maggie Sullivan," he interrupted. "I want to stay with you. I want to spend my life loving and cherishing you as much as I do this second. I want to know when I wake up in the middle of the night I can reach out and find you there. I want to come home to you after a rough day. I want to be there for you when the kids drive you crazy, as I've no doubt Jared does often. I want to see your children grow up and become the best people they can."

He opened the box, pulled out the ring and held it in front of her. It was an antique, platinum setting with an intricately engraved filigreed design. The single carat, heart-shaped diamond in the center was set off by a sapphire baguette on each side.

"Burke." Tears thickened her voice and filled her eyes.

"I want to spend my life with you, the woman who rescued me before I could rescue her. Mags, will you marry me?" He held his grandmother's ring out, waiting eagerly for her answer.

She swallowed deeply as tears streamed down her face. Every nuance of her face was forever ingrained in his memory. Regardless of the next words to come out of her mouth, she'd never looked more beautiful than in this moment. And he knew by her eyes she loved him.

She just had to accept him.

She leaned forward, put her hand on his cheek, kissed him gently, and then laid her cheek against his. His shoulders knotted as he braced for her refusal.

"Marriage," she whispered, "is serious business."

He'd pushed too far, too fast. "I know. I love you. I don't want to live without you."

"I love you." Her warm exhale brushed over his ear, sending goosebumps down his spine. "I don't want to live without you either, Detective Burke Harte. Yes, I'll marry you."

He pulled her closer. His breath swept across her skin. She wiped away tears and pushed away so she was facing him.

"On a couple of conditions," she added.

Nothing came easy. Burke knew the rule, and more precisely the truth of it in relation to women—especially this one. He hated conditions, but for Maggie he was game. "Name them."

"Jared has to agree."

"Logical." He wouldn't love her as much if she didn't think about her kids first. And he could bribe Jared.

"I want the wedding to be small."

"As long as there is one."

"I want it to be soon." She smiled and leaned forward to kiss him.

"I think I can get behind that idea." He pulled a little away, took her left hand and grinned. "You took Mike's ring off."

"It was time."

"Maggie." She'd reached the point of wanting to move on. With him.

She tightened her grip on his hand and shook her head. "Do I get that rock or not?"

He chuckled and nodded. His grin made his cheeks hurt as he slipped on the ring.

She gaped at his ring on her finger and when she looked up, tears shimmered on her eyelashes. Her voice was barely a whisper. "It's gorgeous."

He smiled and ran his thumb under her eyes, gently wiping her tears away. "It was my great-grandmother's. My great-grandfather spent years mining the materials to make this with his own hands. He thought he was being funny when he used a heart in the design."

The tears were now streaming down her face. "I love it even more because of what it means to you. I love you, Burke. You are my heart."

"And you're mine." He kissed the tears from her cheeks, and then slowly rained kisses over her face working his way back to her lips. Giving her one last brief kiss, he pulled away from her. "I can hardly wait until you're Maggie Harte."

"My granddad told me something once before he died." She gripped his hand and squeezed until her knuckles turned white. "Love is the noblest emotion you can feel. It's what gives a man hope, and the courage to not give up. You give me hope and courage, Burke."

And she gave him so much more.

###

About the Author

Heart stopping puppy chases, childhood melodrama and the aborted hangings of innocent toys are all in a day's work for Nikki Duncan. This athletic equestrian turned reluctant homemaker turned daring author, is drawn to the siren song of a fresh storyline.

Nikki plots murder and mayhem over breakfast, scandalous exposés at lunch and the sensual turn of phrase after dinner. Nevertheless, it is the pleasurable excitement and anticipation of unraveling her character's motivation that drives her to write long past the witching hour.

The only anxiety and apprehension haunting this author comes from pondering the mysterious outcome of her latest twist.

More can be found out about Nikki at her website www.NikkiDuncan.com. Nikki is also on Twitter www.twitter.com/nduncanwriter and Facebook at www.facebook.com/nduncanwriter.